THE CU

Colin J Galtrey is riding high in the Amazon best-selling lists for Paperback and E-format.

With twelve Detective John Gammon books and five other books available from other genres. This latest book is the seventeenth book available on Amazon.

I hope you enjoy reading about all the places the books take you to.

A big thank you to everyone who has read the books in whatever format.

Colin J Galtrey.

1

JOHN GAMMON PEAK DISTRICT
DETECTIVE
Series Three Book Two

This book is a work of fiction. Names, characters, organisations, places, events and incidents are either products of the author's imagination or are used fictitiously.
All rights reserved.

No part of this book may be reproduced or stored in a retrieval system or transmitted in any form or by any means, electronic, mechanical, photocopying, recording or otherwise without express permission from the author
C J Galtrey.

THE CURE

A thrilling detective book.

Our hero and his emotions stripped bare.

DI Gammon will go into dark places in his mind and his life as he battles with right and wrong, good and evil.

The Cure is set in the beautiful Peak District of Derbyshire. Many tourists walk the same paths that our hero does. If you are one of them see if you can work out the fictitious villagers and hostelries that Detective Inspector Gammon frequents.
Although Gammon is noted as being an excellent detective, the hierarchy has concerns about his maverick ways. Will this hold him back?

JOHN GAMMON PEAK DISTRICT
DETECTIVE
Series Three Book Two

Contents

THE CURE

CHAPTER ONE

John Gammon knew now that DI Gammon was the best he could hope for, certainly if he stayed at Bixton. That thought didn't endear him to his native county any longer. Saron was not interested, and his best friend was going through so much turmoil, John really needed to think what he wanted.

It had been three months since Gadsby had been found. With the confession about his real mother Gladys Williams, the new guy, DCI Saul Dirk, had taken all the credit for his hard work. But to be fair that is what most senior officers did. DCI Dirk was actually quite ok. He had his moments, but as long as John let him think he was running

the show then he pretty much left
the team to John.

John arrived at Bixton General.
Steve had slept there for three
months while Jo was in recovery.
She still had a long way to go, with
skin grafts etc to try and mend this
poor girl's body. The loss of their
daughter was going to scar them for
the rest of their lives. John headed
for Forest Ward. When he arrived
there was pandemonium. Jo had been
having surgery and her heart had
stopped. Steve was pacing up and
down outside the theatre. Doctors
and nurses were running everywhere.
John didn't know if it was luck that
he arrived in time to be with his
schoolboy friend, but he was glad he
was.

THE CURE

The surgeon came out and asked Steve and John to go into a side office. Steve wouldn't let him speak. He kept saying, "Is she ok?", over and over again.

"Mr Lineman, I am Mr Ralph Frince. I am sorry to inform you, but you wife's heart stopped during surgery and we were unable to revive her. I am very sorry Mr Lineman. Jo was an incredibly brave person, but her body gave up in the end."

Steve broke down. This rufty-tufty man was in pieces. He had lost everything, his home, and now the love of his life. Tracey Rodger, Jo's sister had just arrived as they left the surgeon's small office. She was comforting Steve. John turned to Tracey.

"He can stop at mine as long as he wants."

"John, he will be ok. I have loads of room, and you are at work most of the time. I'll look after him, it's the least I can do for my sister."

Tracey was bearing up quite well and being strong for Steve.

John left the hospital and headed for Bixton Police station. Things had been quiet, but that was about to change.

"Morning Sir."

"Good morning, Sergeant Yap."

"Not for long Sir, DCI Dirk told me this morning that he has the authority to make me up to Detective Sergeant."

"Oh, great news Ian. When will you becoming over to the dark side?" and Gammon laughed.

THE CURE

I think it will be tomorrow. One of the beat lads is coming on as desk sergeant."

"Who's that Ian?"

"Warren Beeney."

"Ok, is DCI Dirk in yet?"

"He was Sir, but after he spoke to me he said he was going to London and to inform you he won't be back this week."

"Great, running the bloody ship again."

Gammon went to his office and did his usual thing if he was stressed. He stood at the widow looking toward Losehill, it seemed to pacify him.

Gammon's phone rang.

"Good morning Detective Inspector Loser," the scrambled voice said.

"Who is this?"

"It doesn't matter who I am. You should be more interested in what I have."

"What is that?"

"A young lady."

"Say hello to Inspector Loser my dear."

"Help me, please help me."

"Ok, so now I have given you proof who I am the guardian of."

"What are you taking about?"

"The young lady you spoke to is my first experiment. I will send you pictures Inspector Loser."

The phone then went dead. What the hell was that all about he thought? As Gammon went to get a coffee Yap was coming up the stairs.

"Sir, I have a lady and a man in interview room one. They are saying their daughter didn't come home last night.

THE CURE

"What's their names Ian?"

"Susan and Jack Toppin. They said they were from Manifold Farm, Hittington."

Gammon knew Susan and Jack, they had been good friends with his mother and father.

Gammon entered the room. Jack was a big powerful man and Susan was a small woman pretty in a plain sort of way.

"Jack, Susan, how are you?"

"Been better John, our daughter Jessie, didn't come home after a night out with friends."

"Has she ever done this before?"

"No John, she is a sensible girl. She is a nurse at Micklock hospital."

"Ok, what about friends or boyfriends? Have you tried contacting them?"

"She was out with some nurses from the hospital; Jane Sharpe, Helen Firm, Lana Crooks and Rachel Yates. We phoned them all and they said that Jessie hadn't been feeling too well so had gone outside to get a taxi home."

"She never arrived home John, I am so worried."

Gammon didn't want to tell them about the call he had taken some time earlier in case it wasn't their daughter.

"Tell me Susan, did she have any boyfriends?"

Yes, she was seeing Mark Block. He is a junior doctor at the hospital."

"Have you spoke to him?"

THE CURE

"No, he was on nights, or he would have probably picked her up."

"Ok, well I'll pop round. Have you got his address?"

"Yes, he lives at Poppy Mill on Beerly Moor."

"Ok, look don't worry, easy for me to say I know, but I am sure she will turn up."

"Thank you, John. We best get back as Jack has sheep to take to market.

The Toppin's left. Although worried, they felt better after hearing Gammon's words. Gammon was concerned about Jessie, so he called DI Lee to go with him to Mark Block's house on Beerly Moor.

Beerly Moor was a bleak area of moorland and Poppy Mill had once been a farm of some substance, with land that covered most of the moor. John knew of it having been there as a little boy with Philip to get hay.

The drive down to the farmhouse was about a quarter of a mile. John wasn't sure if Mr or Mrs Block were still alive. He could only just remember Mr Block anyway.

The farmhouse looked like it had been renovated. It had new windows and doors, and did look quite nice, although a little desolate John thought.

They knocked on the door and after a couple of minutes of knocking a tired looking man came to the door. Gammon estimated he would have been in his late twenties. They both showed their warrant cards as they greeted Mark Block.

"Good morning, Sir."

THE CURE

"Good morning," Block replied looking a little shocked. "How can I help you, officers?"

"I wondered if we could have a word, Sir."

"By all means, please come inside."

Block took them into the big farm house kitchen. It had all been very tastefully decorated.

"Would you both like a coffee?"

"Black, no sugar for me Sir, and what would you like, DI Lee?"

"Could I have a tea please, white, no sugar?"

Block came back with the drinks and they sat at the large kitchen table.

"Now what is this about, Mr Gammon?"

"This morning we had a Mr and Mrs Toppin come to the station to report their daughter missing."

"What Jess?"

"Yes, Mr Block."

"Are you sure? She texted me at midnight to say she was going home as she didn't feel too well."

"Could we see that text please, Mr Block?"

Mark Block showed Gammon and Lee the text. And the reply which Mark had said, "Ok, speak tomorrow."

"So, Mr Block, had you seen Jessie Toppin on the night she disappeared?"

"I saw her for a couple of minutes at work at 7.00pm. I work at the same hospital as Jessie, that's how we met."

"When you say a couple of minutes, can you explain?"

"Yes, she had left her purse in my car by mistake, so she came to the hospital to pick it up."

THE CURE

"How did she seem?"

"Same old Jess. Really Mr Gammon, she is always full of life and a very kind girl. Let me try and ring her mobile while you are here."

Block rang Jessie's number, but it said the phone was switched off.

"Have you spoken with the girls she was going out with?"

"Not yet Mr Block, that's my next port of call."

"Do you live here alone Mr Block?"

"Yes, my parents passed away about five years ago."

"I knew your father, with him being a farmer and my parents had a farm. You never fancied farming then?"

"No, too much like hard work Mr Gammon. I guess you thought the same."

"Yes, my brother went into it, but I never really fancied it has a career. Ok, Mr Block we will be in touch."

"Yes please, let me know. Me and Jess hadn't been going out long, but I would hate anything to have happened to her Mr Gammon."

Gammon and Lee left Poppy Mill. Gammon got DI Lee to get the addresses of the girls that Jessie had been out with, so they could speak with them.

"Ok, let's go and see the girl in the nurse's accommodation at Bixton."

"That's Rachel Yates, Sir."

The accommodation was two storeys in the grounds of the hospital. Rachel lived at number seven. Gammon and Lee climbed the stairs to number seven. DI Lee knocked on the door. A pretty girl answered, she was about twenty three. Gammon and Lee flashed their warrant cards.

"Rachel Yates?"

"Yes, why what's a matter?"

"Could we come in please?"

Yates showed them into a small living room and a young girl was laying on the settee under a sleeping blanket. The girl sat up slightly embarrassed.

"This is Lana Crooks, Mr Gammon. We went out last night, so Lana stayed at mine, because it's easier than going back to Pritwich. We are both on the 2.00pm - 10.00pm shift today."

"Ok, nice to meet you Lana," said Gammon.

"The reason we are here is that it's been reported that Jessie Toppin didn't return home last night."

"I thought that was odd. I tried ringing her, but her phone is off."

"She is off today as she is on nights for a week after that."

"Was Jessie ok last night?"

"To be honest she wasn't herself.. We weren't surprised that she left when she did."

"Had she been arguing with her boyfriend, do you know?"

"I wouldn't have thought so, he is a really nice guy, Mark. I know she thought a lot of him, Mr Gammon."

"Mr Block is a junior doctor, correct?"

"Yes, he works so many hours but then all the juniors do. It's any wonder he has time for a relationship. He is never grumpy though, and he must get tired."

"She will be ok, won't she Mr Gammon?"

THE CURE

"I'm sorry Lana, I can't give you any guarantees. Let's hope so. Did Jessie have any money troubles that you know of?"

"No, her parents looked after her, she is the apple of their eye."

"Ok well thank you Rachel, we will be in touch."

Gammon and Lee left the girls looking frightful.

"Right where next, Peter?"

"Jane Sharpe, 14 Riber Crescent, John. I think that is on the new estate. Drive up there we will find it."

The estate was only about a year old. It was a mix of starter homes and three bed-roomed semi-detached. 14 Riber Crescent was a starter home. Gammon and Lee proceeded to the front door. A young lady was just coming out.

"Miss Sharpe?"

Jane Sharpe was startled, "Yes."

"DI Lee and DI Gammon, Bixton Police, could we have a word?"

"I'm sorry but I will be late for my bus to the hospital."

"We can take you and talk on the way."

Sharpe scrutinised the warrant cards before getting in the car with Gammon and Lee. Gammon sat in the back and was asking Jane Sharpe the same questions he had asked her friends. He wanted to know if she thought Mark Block was as nice as the others said. To Gammon's surprise Sharpe said he was a really nice bloke. She had dated him two year earlier, but she had finished the relationship because he was always at work.

"He is a nice guy though, Mr Gammon."

THE CURE

"How did you feel when Jessie Toppin started seeing him?"

"Not a problem to me. We have been mates since the start of nursing college, and I had moved on anyway."

"Ok, well if you can think of anything that might help find Jessie please get in touch," and Gammon handed her his card.

"Ok Peter, let's go and speak with Helen Firm. She lives in Bixton."

"Ok, what's the address?

"The Cottage, Lowly Hill. That's only just outside Bixton, Peter. Come on I will show you."

Gammon instructed DI Lee as they left the hospital and headed for Lowly Hill. It took about ten minutes before they arrived at the cottage. Gammon knocked on the

door. A guy in his mid thirties
answered.

"DI Gammon and Lee," John said
showing both their warrant cards.

"What do you want?"

The man wasn't the most gracious
of characters.

"We would like to speak with
Miss Firm."

"She ain't no miss, it's Mrs Firm,
my wife. What do you want with
her?"

It was clear that Firm wasn't
going to allow them into the
cottage.

"We are investigating a missing
person."

"Well that was bloody quick. I
haven't reported her missing yet."

"I'm sorry, we are investigating
her friend Jessie Toppin, not your
wife. Are you saying your wife is
missing?"

THE CURE

"Either that, or she copped off with some random bloke last night."

"You don't seem to upset about it Mr Firm."

"We are about to split up, so it dunna matter now."

"So, you are saying your wife Helen didn't come home last night?"

"He's bloody bright, ain't he?"

Gammon could see DI Lee wasn't happy with Firm's comment.

"Mr Firm, you appear very blasé about your wife's disappearance. If I was you I would have a bit more sense she may be in danger."

"Could not give a toss, copper. Now if you done with me, I'll get on," and Firm showed them the door.

"What's your Christian name, Mr Firm?"

"John, why are you going to run me through your bloody computer?"

Gammon and Lee got back in the car.

"I don't like him, John."

"Well I have to agree Peter, not the nicest of characters. Let's hope she has just left him."

They arrived back at Bixton and Gammon met Steve coming out of the station.

"You ok mate?"

"Yeah, just popped in to tell you Jo's funeral will be on Monday next week at Hittington Church, mate. I'm going to bury alongside our daughter."

"Are you ok, mate?"

"Yeah fine, John. Best rush mate, Tracey is waiting for me."

Gammon entered the station.

THE CURE

"Sir, this is Warren Beeney, our new desk sergeant. He is training this week."

"Pleased to meet you Sergeant Beeney."

"So, you are coming over to the dark side next week, are you Ian?"

"Yes Sir, can't wait."

Gammon smiled and climbed the stairs. He grabbed a coffee and Di Scooper was passing with a piece of chocolate cake she had made for DI Smarty's birthday. She plonked a chunk on a paper plate and gave it to John.

"Thanks, Sandra. Excuse me the phone's ringing."

"Hello, DI Gammon speaking."

"Mr Gammon, you got the girl yet?"

"Who is this?"

"You can call me MM if you wish. The girl, Jessie Toppin, is in

the bushes by the café in the park in
Micklock. Will have another to test
your forensic lads shortly John,"
and telephone went dead.

Gammon decided to call DCI
Dirk and fill him in on what had
happened so far. Much as he didn't
want to, he thought it best to keep
him sweet.

Dirk told Gammon that he would
be back the following Monday and
to arrange a meeting for everyone in
the incident room to see what he
had. Gammon had told DI Milton
and Sergeant Magic to go with
forensics to the café in the park at
Micklock to see if there was a body.

Milton confirmed there was, so
Gammon decided to drive down to
Manifold Farm in Hittington to
speak with Jack and Susan Toppin.

THE CURE

It was a wet and quite bleak night which added to the empty feeling John had on these occasions. The farmyard was quite muddy, and he could see the milking parlour lights were on. He parked outside the kitchen window where he could see Susan Toppin through the checked curtains. John knocked on the door. Susan answered the door.

"Hello John, come in. I am just making a stew and dumplings. Jack loves his dumplings. Have you any news?"

"Get Jack, Mary, I want to talk to both of you."

Mary shouted across the yard and Jack came over. He reminded John so much of Phil. You could smell the cow muck as it wafted round the kitchen.

"Now lad, any news?"

"I'm afraid we have found a body, and the killer contacted me and said it was your daughter."

Poor Susan almost fainted. Jack held her steady.

"I am so sorry."

"What happened?"

"All we know at this stage is her body was found at the café in the park in Micklock late this afternoon after I took a call from the likely killer. I am so sorry for your loss, but I do have to ask you to come down in the morning at 11.00am to identify the body."

"Do you need a grief counsellor?"

"No, we will be fine lad. You get on your way and let me and her mother grieve in private. I will come and identify the body in the morning at time you said lad."

"Ok, Jack, Susan I will bid you goodnight."

THE CURE

John walked back to his car. Deep inside he felt like screaming. Why would anybody kill and innocent girl?

It was now 6.10pm and John rang Steve.

"Hello mate, do you want to come for a drink?"

"No, I'm ok mate, just watching the news with Tracey and she is cooking tea."

John decided to go and see Kev. Maybe he could cheer him up. On the way Milton called. He said there had been no witnesses, but Wally had said she had been in the bushes maybe an hour.

"How can there be no witnesses, Carl. It's a busy park."

"I know but we haven't been able to find anybody that saw anything."

"Ok, against my better judgement get radio Derby to appeal for witnesses."

"Ok John, see you in the morning."

John arrived to see Kev beaming behind the bar of the Spinning Jenny.

"What are you looking so chuffed about mate?"

"We have won Peak District pub of the year mate."

"Wow, well done Kev. So, is it a big prize?"

"Yeah, it's taken on food, beer and hospitality. I always wanted to win it John."

"You have been away, haven't you?"

"Yes, had a break in Stratford. Only got back about an hour ago and I was met with the good news."

THE CURE

"Pleased for you Kev."

"What are you drinking?"

"Pedigree please, Bud."

"How's Steve and Jo bearing up? Must have been awful losing the little one and then Steve having to do the funeral on his own."

He doesn't know John thought.

"Jo died Kev, on the operating table. The funeral is Monday."

"Oh hell, I didn't know John. How is he? That's dreadful for the lad."

"I think he is in shock, he just seems normal."

"Do you think I should call him? Me and Doreen will be at the funeral."

"Probably not Kev. I would imagine everyone is calling him."

They both tried to lighten the mood, but it wasn't going to

happen. John only had a couple and left.

When he arrived home there was a letter from Fleur. John hurriedly opened the letter from his half-sister.

'Dear John

Just a quick letter. I hope you had a nice Christmas and I guess you are a married man now. Sorry I didn't get there, but you know how my job is.

I have news about Saskia Wagers. She is alive so your friend did see her. Obviously you must not let him know who told you. From what I am told she is in a safe house in a village called Pommie. She hasn't had to go far since her death was faked.

Do as you wish with this information, but I trust you to burn this letter.

THE CURE

I look forward to seeing you sometime soon. Would be lovely to have time with you and your new wife.

I will be in touch soon
Love
Fleur xx'

John did as his sister had said and burned the letter in the log burner. Now his dilemma was whether to tell Carl or not. He decided that the day after tomorrow, Saturday, he would trace her and maybe have a word before deciding. If she wanted Carl to know then he would tell him. But if she didn't then he would let sleeping dogs lay he thought.

John was up and in work for 8.10am to make sure he had everybody ready for the meeting in the incident room at 9.00am. When

he arrived DI Milton, DI Scooper
and DI Smarty were already in.
What a dedicated team he thought
as he climbed the stairs to his office.

At 8.50am his phone rang. It was
the killer again.

"Got your second one, John. Have
a look in Mowstone Quarry near
Pommie. I was nearly disturbed, so
I had to just let her go in the big
hole, but she is there for you. I will
make it easy. Her name is Maga
Wuxi, she was a law student. I
chose to see if her body reacted
differently. Anyway John, let you
get on. I'm sure you are trying to
find me."

Gammon asked IT if they could
trace the calls he had on his mobile,
but the caller had somehow blocked
so there was no trace. He headed
down for the incident room
meeting.

THE CURE

Everybody was assembled.

"Ok, if you could tell us what you found please, Wally."

"The lady, we believe to be Jessie Toppin," and Wally pointed at the photograph on the board.

"She appears to have died from bleach poisoning."

There was a gasp from the collected team.

"Had she not died of this, she would have almost certainly died from liver failure caused by hepatitis. From my investigations it appears that somebody was experimenting with neat bleach injected into the blood stream to see if it would attack the virus.

There is no sign of any sexual contact prior to her death and there was only bruising on her arm from injections. We did find small amounts of chloroform in her system which may have been used to sedate her."

"Thank you, Wally. Mr and Mrs Toppin will be here at 11.00am to identify their daughter's body."

"Ok everyone, a few minutes before the meeting I took a phone call from our killer. The man told me that he had murdered a Chinese student who was studying at Derby University. Her name is Maga Wuxi. He has told me her threw down Mowstone Quarry which is a disused quarry near the village of Pommie. I have sent a rescue team to recover her body and the forensic team I need some answers on this by tomorrow morning."

"It's Saturday, John."

"I know, I will be in for the results please, Wally."

Wally was left with no illusion that Gammon wanted results.

THE CURE

Gammon climbed the stairs grabbing a coffee before entering his office. He had just sat down when DI Smarty came in.

"Have you got a minute, John?"

"Yes, grab a seat Dave, what's the problem?"

"No problem John."

"Not long after I moved up here we rented a cottage from a Chris Pope. He was retired and he owned three cottages. This guy was really interesting. He had climbed all over the world with some of the top climbers during the mid-seventies. He was a nice guy and I remember him telling me a story about a suicide pact in the Peak District. The story went that three nineteen year old lads and three girls aged eighteen had got into some kind of witchcraft type thing. He said they were all on magic mushrooms at the time."

"So why are you telling me this Dave?"

"Well the leader, a David Sowers, had a fixation in bleach. He had told them in order to cleanse themselves they should all take a swig of bleach. It killed Margaret Summers, Yvette Wyn, Donald Black and Ivan Wilson. Sowers and his girlfriend Jackie Bush survived because they drank from a different bottle which had grapefruit, not bleach, in it.

At their trial Sowers and Bush said they were convinced that bleach one day would be used in medicine. They got thirty years. Both were freed about eight years ago and guess what they live in the Peak District."

THE CURE

"Bloody hell Dave, brilliant mate. Find out where they live and let's have them in for questioning."

"Will do John."

Smarty left John to sort Sowers and Bush. Gammon carried on with his paperwork mindful that although it was Saturday tomorrow he needed the results from Wally. Then he was going to see Steve about the funeral arrangements. Not something he was looking forward to, but he needed to be there for his mate. He had then decided to go to Pommie to see if he could find Saskia Wagers. Then if he could, he had to make a decision with Carl.

It was 5.10pm when John was just turning the light off in his office and calling it a night, when Smarty stopped him.

"Found them John. I'll bring them in for questioning on Monday."

JOHN GAMMON PEAK DISTRICT
DETECTIVE
Series Three Book Two

"Great work Dave. Have a nice weekend."

"You too, John."

Gammon left Smarty beaming that he had come up with these suspects. He could feel the pull of the Spinning Jenny has he drove from Bixton.

He arrived at the pub some thirty minutes later

It was almost 5.40pm when John walked down the stone steps to the bar area. There were just a couple of walkers sat by the fire and Anouska behind the bar.

"Hello handsome," she said in a very sexy manner. Anouska was dressed in her usual rock chick outfit that left little to the imagination.

"I'll have a Pedigree please."

THE CURE

"John, I heard about your friend so sad, and the baby was lost in the fire. How tragic."

"Yes, poor Steve will need a lot of support."

John felt a tap on his shoulder and turned around to see Sheba Filey with Phil Sterndale.

"Hi John, sorry to hear about Jo and the baby. How's Steve?"

Phil Sterndale thrust out his hand for John to shake.

"Sorry to hear about your friend's problems, and I want to thank you for finding those low lives out."

John shook his hand.

Phil had bought back his parent's land and the rights to the building work.

"John, quite exciting times thanks to you sorting that crew out."

"Well I didn't do it on my own, we are a team at Bixton."

"All the same Mr Gammon I have no hard feelings. You had to investigate everyone, and I guess at some point I would have been the prime suspect, so I hope we can be friends."

"I won't be a second, Sheba. I need to go to the little boy's room."

Sterndale left John and Sheba talking.

"I thought you were quite big friends with Linda Sterndale, Phil's wife, Sheba?"

"We were, but I actually knew Phil before Linda. When it all kicked off he had been going through a terrible time with his parents selling his inheritance so cheaply. Then he was a suspect in the murder case, and he just isn't like that. Phil and Linda were having problems in their marriage, and she then accused me of seeing him. I wasn't at the time I was just being a good mate. Anyway, he asked me out as they have totally split now, and I thought what the hell John?"

"Well I hope it works out for you both."

John had two more drinks then left knowing he had to be back at work Saturday morning for the results from Wally. He also had to go and see Steve about the funerals of Jo and baby Leah Marie.

The following morning Wally met John at the station.

"John, the victim was indeed a young girl called Maga Wuxi. We confirmed it through dental records. She was from Shenzhen in China, and she was an exchange student. We found needle marks on her arm and she had been administered

sodium hypochlorite, or as you may
know it bleach. Without being too
technical John, it's produced by
passing chlorine gas through dilute
sodium hydroxide."

"Ok Wally, I don't want the labour
pains, just the baby. How much
bleach was found inside the poor
girl?"

"I think she had three injections of
the bleach. Very small amounts, but
enough to kill her, John. She had not
been sexual assaulted in any way,
it's purely the bleach. There were
signs of bruising on her neck, and I
am guessing she was drugged when
she was abducted."

"Any DNA?"

"Yes, we found a small amount of
DNA on a handbag. We checked the
police database, and we got a match
to an Andrew Gilbon. He works as a
janitor at the university, John."

THE CURE

"Great, well done Wally, and thanks for coming in today."

"No problem John. It got me out of shopping," and Wally laughed.

John called DI Milton and the new DS Yap and told them to find out where Gilbon lived, and basically stake him out over the weekend.

With enough done at work he headed to see Steve, not something he was looking forward to. The funeral was on Monday so he needed to see how he was.

John arrived at Tracey Rodger's house which was unaffected by the fire. She met John at the door and showed him in. Tracey had clearly been very upset. Steve on the other hand seemed ok. He had all the plans for the funerals of Jo and his daughter. John was quite surprised how strong he seemed.

"Jo loved this hymn, John."

"Oh, 'There is a Green Hill'. I like that also. What about the other hymn?"

"I'm going for 'Morning has Broken'."

"Lovely mate. Tracey and I are doing the eulogies."

"She wanted to be buried in Hittington church yard, so they will both be buried there, mate. Coming into church to 'Have I Told You Lately that I Love You' by Rod Stewart and then leaving church will be 'Photograph' by Ed Sheeran. She loved that."

John could see Steve was ok. He was looking through pictures of Jo when she was a girl. Tracey said he could have some, as all Steve's pictures were burnt in the fire.

John could see Steve was in his own world, so he said he would see him at church on Monday.

THE CURE

John left and headed to Pommie to see if there was any chance he could find Saskia Wagers and see if she wanted Carl to get in contact.

The best place for information is the local pub. The Farmers Inn was in the centre of the village of Pommie.

Pommie was quite a spread-out village of farms and quarrymen cottages. It had three pubs The Farmers, The Black Bull and The Pommie Arms.

This wasn't going to be easy John thought, as he couldn't really ask after Beth because she was probably calling herself by another name.

John got talking to two local lads and decided to mention what Beth looked like. He made the pretence that he was over from America and his family tree led him to Pommie and the name Wagers. One of the lads said there was a Beth Wagers who worked behind the bar at the Pommie Arms. She's a right cracker he said, but she won't go out with anyone. This made John smile, so he made his excuses and left. He headed down the cobbled street towards the Pommie Arms hoping she might be working.

It was now 5.50pm and there was a guy behind the bar. John overheard him say Beth was taking him off at 6.00pm, so he got his pint and sat in the corner and waited.

Sure enough Beth appeared just before 6.00pm. John waited for the guy to leave and that left just him and Beth in the pub. Perfect he thought.

John finished his pint and headed for the bar. The look on Beth's face as she remembered John. She tried to put her head down as she served him.

John didn't want to frighten the girl, but a promise was a promise and so he asked her outright about Carl.

Beth looked at John and a small tear ran down her cheek.

"I will tell the boss I'm not very well and we can talk."

Beth disappeared into a back room and came back with her coat on.

"Quickly, meet me outside."

Beth came out and they wandered down the cobbled street turning left by the church. At the back of the churchyard was a small detached cottage.

"Come in and I will explain."

Beth's cottage was small but neat. She poured two glasses of red wine and they sat at the kitchen table.

"How did you find me?"

"I have ways, but more importantly, why did you let Carl see you?"

Beth hesitated for a short time.

"I know I shouldn't have, but I can't help it. I am so lonely. I found out where he was, and I purposely wanted to see him, but I bottled it at the last minute. When my protection officer found out he wasn't best pleased, and they moved me overnight. In fact they moved me twice."

"Why stay in the Peak District though Beth?"

"This was my only stipulation. I said I was staying and Pommie seemed ideal."

"The million-dollar question now Beth. Do you want Carl to know? If it's yes, then I will tell him. If it's no, then I will respect your wishes."

THE CURE

Beth asked John for his number as she wanted to think about it. She said she didn't want to put Carl in any danger. She had been warned that the people chasing her would not give up if they believed she was alive.

John gave her his number, thanked her for the wine and said he looked forward to hearing from her. He left the little cottage and returned to his car.

He had three missed calls all from Saron. Strange John thought. He tried to ring her back but it went to answer phone, so he decided to call at the Tow'd Man.

Saron was sitting at the bar when he walked in, He sensed she was a little bit tipsy. Donna Fringe was working the bar and there were a few locals, but not many as it was now 10.30pm.

"Hi Saron, I have been trying to call you back."

"What are you drinking John?"

"I'll have a large brandy. What about Saron?"

"Same for me please, John."

"Take one for yourself, Donna."

"The reason I called you was to ask you what time the funeral is?"

"10.30am at Hittington Church."

"Could I be cheeky and come with you, John? I really don't like funerals and especially if I go on my own."

"Yes of course you can."

John felt quite elated that she wanted to go with him.

After a couple more drinks Saron told John she was calling it a night.

"Donna I'm off to bed. It's been a long day, anymore and I won't be up. I have sixty five for Sunday lunch tomorrow."

THE CURE

Saron said goodnight to John and he said he would pick her up at 9.50am Monday morning and to be ready.

John had one more drink and sat chatting with Donna.

"How's the station doing John?"

"I thought you would have got the DCI job."

"Ruffled too many feathers over the years. The new guy is Saul Dirk. He is ok to be fair, pretty much lets me get on with it. Think he is more interested in motorbikes than he is policing," and John laughed.

"How are you finding pub life?"

"Probably not quite what I expected. It's very hard work John. I don't know how Saron does it to be honest. Will you two sort things out, do you think?"

"I would like to Donna but not sure she can forgive me."

"Well you never know. Look John, I'm not being funny but it's been a long day, so I am going to shut."

"No problem Donna, was nice to have a chat."

THE CURE

CHAPTER TWO

John arrived back at his cottage mindful that Steve had asked him to say something at Jo and baby Leah's funerals on the Monday.

He poured a large Jameson's and sat by his log stove with a pad and pen. John wrote down the words he intended to use at the funeral. He spent almost two hours before he finally was happy with the eulogy and he headed to bed.

The following morning John didn't wake until 10.00am which was really unusual. John's phone had three calls from DS Yap.

He called Yap back and apologised for missing the previous three calls.

"What's the problem Ian?"

"We staked out Andrew Gilbon last night. Around 2.00am he left his house and at 3.11am he returned to his house with a young lady. She hasn't left yet and we are not sure if we should leave Sir, as it's now been fourteen hours."

"Ok Ian, give me half an hour and I will come and relieve you and Carl."

John quickly changed and headed for 14 Haddon Walk, Dilley Dale. Yap and Milton looked tired, so John quickly got the information from them and told them to leave the stake out tonight and go to work as normal Monday.

John settled in his car at a safe distance from the property. Nothing happened until 3.00pm. Then all hell broke loose. John could hear screaming so he rushed to the front door of the property.

"Police, let me in," he asked twice. Then kicked the door in. Gammon found Gilbon in a corner and the woman with a stiletto shoe hitting him and screaming. Gammon flashed his warrant card and had already called for back-up. He restrained the woman then realised she was Jane Sharpe a friend of one of the victims, Helen Firm.

"That's enough, Miss Sharpe."

Gammon restrained Sharpe. Andrew Gilbon stood up. He had blood pouring down his face from two cuts; one on his head and another above his right eye.

Back-up arrived, and Gammon sent Gilbon to hospital with two beat lads, and instructions to bring him to the station once he was sorted. He then arranged for Jane Sharpe to be taken to the station so he could question her. Gammon followed in his car.

He rang the new desk Sergeant,
Warren Beeney, to get a search
warrant in place for Gilbon's house
and car. He instructed him to get DS
Magic and DI Lee in to oversee it.

Gammon arrived at Bixton station
and Sergeant Beeney said Sharpe
was in interview room two with DI
Scooper who had been in work.
Gammon went in and Scooper
started the tape.
"Miss Sharpe, may I call you
Jane?"
"Yes, not a problem."
"Ok, so tell me in your own words
what happened tonight?"
"I was stood waiting for a taxi
from Christies in Ackbourne when
Andrew Gilbon pulled up and
offered me a lift. I knew Andrew and
he always seemed a decent guy. He
was quite friendly with Helen Firm."

THE CURE

"Let me stop you there, Jane. I thought Helen was married."

"Well she is, but only really in name. She couldn't afford a place on her own, so she stuck it with that jerk."

"The jerk being her husband Andrew, correct?"

"Yes."

"Ok, so you are not a fan?"

"No way, Jose."

"So, you get in the car with Mr Gilbon."

"He said he was going back to Dilley Dale, which is on the way to Bixton, and it would save me money, so I said yes. On the way he seemed a really nice guy. He asked me if I fancied a coffee."

"Did you not think it was a bit dangerous, knowing what happened to your friend Jane?"

"I represented England at kick boxing two years ago, and although I don't train or fight now I can look after myself."

"Ok Jane, so you enter the house?"

"Yes, then he asked if I wanted a glass of wine or a coffee. I had a glass of wine. He put some music on and to be honest I quite fancied him, he is very good looking."

"So, what went wrong?"

"Well, he kissed me, which is fine, but then he called me Helen. I was annoyed; first that he got my name wrong and then that he was calling me by my dead friend's name."

"I was furious, but he tried it on, and wouldn't take no for an answer. So, I dropped him then. I picked up one of my shoes that I had taken off and I hit him twice just to show him

THE CURE

I meant business. That's when you came crashing in."

"Ok, was Andrew Gilbon aggressive also?"

"I didn't give him chance Mr Gammon, bloody pervert."

"Do you wish to press charges, and bear in mind that Mr Gilbon may wish too?"

"What can he press charges on me defending myself?"

"It will be your word against his Jane."

"I just want to go home and forget the whole incident."

"Ok Jane, I will be in touch."

Jane Sharpe left Bixton Police Station and only a few minutes later Gilbon arrived having been stitched up. Gammon kept the same room for Gilbon's interview.

DI Scooper started the tape.

"Mr Gilbon, or may I call you Andrew?"

"Fine by me."

"Just so you know, we found small traces of your DNA on a murder victim, Maga Wuxi, a Chinese student from Derby University, so we have been watching your movements."

Gilbon didn't look as cock sure of himself after the revelation from Gammon.

"I want my lawyer."

"Not a problem Mr Gilbon. I suggest we keep you overnight. Then you contact your lawyer in the morning and we can carry on with the interview.

"Interview suspended until 9.30am tomorrow."

"Take Mr Gilbon to a holding cell until the morning please, DI Scooper."

THE CURE

After Scooper had taken Gilbon down she said she was heading home.

"John, I have just realised it's Jo's funeral tomorrow, I was hoping to go."

"No worries, I have told DI Trimble to get DI Lee and Sergeant Magic to take the interview. I have scribbled down some points, but will ring DI Lee tomorrow morning."

"You don't fancy escorting me to the funeral tomorrow, do you?"

"Well I would, but Saron has asked if I would go with her."

"Oh, back in favour are we?"

Sandra laughed as she left John and headed home.

The following morning John dressed in his black Versace suit. He called it his funeral suit, he never wore it any other time. He had a white shirt that Phyllis Swan, his cleaner, had ironed and hung up for him. She had even gone to the trouble of polishing his shoes.

John arrived at the Tow'd Man at 9.45am. Saron was ready as always. She looked stunning in a black Stella McCartney dress cut just above the knee. With black Christian Le Boutin shoes and a black small cropped jacket. She had a single strand of cultured pearls to emphasise her beautiful neck and skin.

She pecked John on the cheek and she had her smell, just a hint of Chanel No 5. They arrived at Hittington Church. It was now 10.15am and they were shown to seats at the front. John had his eulogy safe in his pocket. At almost 10.30am, with the church packed and people standing outside, Steve came in carrying Jo's coffin with three

THE CURE

men from the funeral directors. Little Leah Marie's coffin was already at the front. Steve had asked John to help carry the coffin, but he said he preferred to do a eulogy. Steve said he understood things were still quite raw having lost all his family.

Saron gripped John's arm as they played the Rod Stewart song 'Have I told you lately that I love you'.

Steve helped place the coffin and came and stood next to Tracey, his sister in law, John and Saron. Steve seemed surprisingly calm, but John knew the signs, he had always been like that has a kid. If he was upset he would seem calm inside, then whoosh he would go off like a bottle of pop.

The vicar stood up in the pulpit.

"We are here today to support Steven in his anguish at losing Jo and baby Leah Marie.

At times like this we question our faith. But our faith is what will get Steven through these dark days. I know his friends John, Jack, Bob, Kevin, and so many more will be there for Steven.

Steven told me how Jo was the love of his life. How when he met her, as he put it, he could have done cart wheels all the way through Pritwich. Steven told me that Jo changed his life. He had been in the Navy and meeting Jo gave him a new purpose.

The house they shared was magnificent, and they had both worked so hard to achieve its natural glory.

When Jo said she was pregnant Steven told me that he was the luckiest man alive, they idolised little Leah Marie.

THE CURE

Could you all stand for the first hymn 'There is a Green Hill Far Away'."

The congregation stood and sang. Saron was weeping and holding tight to John's arm. Once they had finished the vicar asked everybody to be seated. John could hear women crying and men sniffling. Still Steve seemed ok, although poor Tracey Rodgers was in bits.

The vicar started talking.

"We often say that God moves in mysterious ways. At times even I wonder why things happen, but we are all part of a bigger plan. Our bodies are merely vehicles that take us through our daily life, until we are called to be with our father.

Many years ago, when I was training for my vocation, I questioned a man who had been a vicar for almost fifty years. The man was almost eighty nine years old. He said our Father only takes the ones that are ready for his kingdom. When I asked why he was still here, he said that he was our Father's voice on this earth.

I thought about it that night and thought about all the really nice people who had appeared to be taken early, yet some bad people I had met were still around. Then it began to make sense."

"Would you please stand for our second hymn? 'Morning Has Broken'."

Again the congregation sang with gusto. Steve was still bearing up.

After the hymn had been sung he made his way to the pulpit. Steve cleared his throat.

"First of all I want to thank you from the bottom of my heart for coming here today, and for your kind words of support for me.

What can I say about our little girl? She had a smile so infectious you were consumed by it. When you met her she was the prettiest thing, just like her Mum. I am sure her Mummy is holding her little hand looking down on us today. Go on your journey my beautiful baby girl and one day we will be together again.

Jo Wickets what a lovely name. My Jo she was vivacious, stunningly beautiful, kind and caring. I had to pinch myself every day that I spent with her.

Jo made broken look beautiful, she walked with the universe on her shoulders and made it look like wings."

That was the point that Steve broke down. Tracey Rodgers rushed to the pulpit and she led him back to the pew. The vicar gestured to John to go to the pulpit.

John also cleared his throat and stood for a minute looking at his best mate totally distraught in the pew below.

"Life is but a stopping place. A pause in time for what we are meant to be.

We all have different journeys and Jo and Leah Marie have started on theirs.

Their destination is far greater than we can imagine. I am sure Jo and Leah Marie would not want Steve to carry the burden of sorrow.

I am sure that their time seemed all too brief, but I am also sure knowing Jo as I did that, she would not want untold grief.

To a dear friend and Steve and Jo's beautiful daughter you will always be in our thoughts. Our Lord will take care of you."

John left the pulpit with tears streaming down his cheeks. He could see Steve had composed himself.

The vicar returned to the pulpit.

"Ladies and Gentlemen, Steven has asked me to thank you all for coming. He knows some of you have had far to travel, in particular Jo's Uncle Mick and Aunty Beryl, who have come from Canada to pay their respects. Steven also asked me to tell everyone that they are welcome to attend at the Spinning Jenny public house in Swinster for drinks and food to celebrate Jo and Leah Marie's life.

Any of the close family that wish to attend the graveside with Steven are more than welcome."

The bearers picked up the coffin
and Steve had asked John to carry
Leah Marie while he was one of the
bearers for Jo's coffin.

They left the church to the song
'Photograph' by Ed Sheeran.

There were a dozen people round
the grave that had been dug earlier in
the day.

"We gather today at the final
resting place of Jo and Leah Marie.
We have full knowledge of the
journey they are taking to be at the
side of our Lord.

In honour of Jo and Leah Marie I
will now recite the final prayer to
consecrate their grave and commit
their spirits to everlasting life. In
sure and certain hope of the
resurrection to eternal life through
our Lord Jesus Christ we commend
to Almighty God. Jo and Leah
Marie. We commit their bodies to

the ground. Earth to earth, ashes to ashes, dust to dust. The Lord bless them and keep them that they have everlasting life. Amen."

Steve threw the first soil on the coffin, with Tracey the second then John and Saron followed by the rest of the graveside mourners.

The day had brightened up it was as if they Jo had opened the curtains has the clouds parted and a bright ray of sunshine engulfed the grave-side.

John took Saron who was still upset back to the Spinning Jenny. On the way she said she could not believe that they had lost Jo and Leah Marie.

The Spinning Jenny was packed, and Doreen had out on a spread of some magnitude. Steve was going around everyone so John left him to it. He seemed to be coping and he

would be there for him in the future
dark days ahead.

It was almost 5.00pm when DI
Smarty arrived.

"I didn't know that you knew Jo,
Dave."

"Can I have a word John?"

He took John to one side.

"What is it Dave, if its work can't
it wait until the morning?"

"John, we have just had the report
from the fire service they believe the
fire was started deliberately."

"What, you are kidding me?"

"No, sorry I'm not mate."

"Oh crap, look Dave we will
discuss this tomorrow together."

"Yes, no problem John just
thought you should know mate."

"I appreciate that, Dave."

John went back to Saron who was
now talking to Steve. John found it

hard to look Steve in the eye
knowing what he had just been told.

"Thanks for today John, that was a
lovely speech."

"Hey not a problem, so have you
got any plans now."

"Well I am stopping in the lodge
which Tracey kindly let me stay."

"Well, technically it is your house
I guess Steve."

"Well I suppose so but it's big
enough for us both to live there for
now."

"I just feel so bad about our
relationship in the weeks before she
died, John."

"Hey, listen mate we all go
through trauma in our relationships."

"You can say that again John,"
said Saron.

"So, are you two back together,
John?"

"Umm no, not really are we Saron?"

"No, we aren't Steve."

"Whoops mate, dropped you in it there."

"I'll let you off Steve."

By 9.00pm there was only Tracey Rodgers, Steve, John, Saron and Jo's relations from Canada. DI Scooper hadn't come to the wake.

John ordered six double brandies and raised a toast to Jo and Leah Marie.

"I need to go back Tracey."

"Well that's lucky, because I ordered a taxi before John got the last drink, and he has just pulled up on the car-park."

Steve and Tracey and the Canadian relations that were staying at the lodge all left. Kev poured him, Doreen, John and Saron another brandy while Saron ordered a taxi.

THE CURE

"I was surprised Jeanette wasn't there, John."

"I guess since her mum had not been well all the work falls on her shoulders."

"I haven't heard from Jeanette in ages. I really should pop down and see her Doreen."

"Right, are you ready?"

Saron was putting her coat on.

"See you two soon."

"I'm sure you will John, take care love. Lovely to see you Saron."

"Likewise, nice to see you, Kev and Doreen."

They climbed in the back of the taxi.

"Are you staying at mine Saron?"

She hesitated then said, "If you want me to, John."

"Your cottage then Mr Gammon," the taxi driver said with a wry smile that needed no explanation.

He dropped them at the cottage
and they went in. Saron was a bit
tipsy.

"Shall we have a night cap,
Saron?"

"Ok, where are we sleeping?"

John could not believe his luck.

"Top of the stairs. on the left. I'll
bring the brandy up."

Saron carefully climbed the stairs
in the cottage. John poured the
brandies and followed her, but by the
time he arrived she was fast asleep.

John looked at her. She was like a
Princess and he was certainly the
frog he thought. He carefully slipped
into bed so as not to wake her, but
half hoping she would wake up.

John was also soon asleep and the
following morning when he woke
Saron had gone leaving a note on the
kitchen table.

THE CURE

'Sorry John, I got Donna to pick me up and I organised a taxi for 8.30am to pick you up for your car. Thank you for getting me here safe. It was an emotional day and maybe that got to me a bit. I really should have told the taxi driver to drop me at the Tow'd Man. Thank you for being a gentleman x'

John was a bit upset but not actually surprised after what he did. All he could do he thought was try harder.

The taxi arrived, and John picked his car up from the Spinning Jenny. On the way into work he was intrigued by what DI Smarty had said at the funeral and was keen to look into it.

"Morning Sergeant Beeney, is DI Smarty in yet?"

"Yes Sir, just arrived."

"Ok, thanks Sergeant."

Gammon made his way to Smarty's office.

"Morning Dave, what was all that about at the funeral yesterday?"

"Well the Fire Service lads thought it was a bit odd, so they reported it. I sent John Walvin and his crew to have a look round knowing everyone would have been at the funeral."

"So, what did they find?"

"The pipe leading to the gas cooker had been slightly cut, John."

"Well that could have been there forever. It doesn't mean it's been cut deliberately."

"Well Wally thinks it was, and he wants permission to cordon off the site and do some proper research."

"I don't want to say this John, but your mate is the prime suspect."

THE CURE

"I need to bring him in for questioning."

"DCI Dirk got a whiff of it and wants to be in on the interview."

"Well if anybody is bringing him in it's me. I owe him that much Dave."

"Your choice, John."

"Dirk is in late this morning, so it will give you time to get up there and talk with him before you bring him in."

John left Bixton station knowing this could potentially ruin a friendship. Bloody job he thought as he drove to the lodge. Here is a man that has only just buried his wife and daughter, and I am going to bring him in for questioning, and tell him he is a suspect in what might be a murder!

Steve was just about to get in his car when John pulled up.

"Hey mate, you come for a coffee? I would ask Tracey to make a breakfast, but she has gone to do some hours for Saron."

"No, actually mate can we go inside and I will have that coffee?"

"Yeah sure, you look serious, are you ok?"

Gammon didn't answer.

Steve poured two coffees and they sat at the kitchen table.

"Look mate, this is as hard for me as it is for you."

"What are you on about, John?"

"I'm afraid one of my colleagues got the fire report yesterday and the Fire Service are treating the chip pan fire as suspicious."

"What?"

"Apparently the hose leading to the cooker had been slit and they found traces of barbecue starter fuel."

THE CURE

Steve looked ashen and was shaking his head.

"The problem is Steve, my boss DCI Dirk wants the house cordoning off today as a potential crime scene. There is nothing I can do."

"Did you know about this on the day of the funeral? I saw that copper come and say something to you and then go."

"Until he came to see me I didn't know anything, and it was your wife's and baby's funeral. I wasn't going to let them do anything."

"Like what John?"

"I am afraid I have to take you in for questioning."

"This is bloody ridiculous."

"Look I know mate, but I don't have a choice. I am sure there will be a perfectly good explanation."

Gammon told Steve to get his coat
and he would drive him to the
station.

There was very little said in the
car. Steve was very quiet, and
Gammon felt terrible. This man had
always had his back right from
junior school, and now he was taking
him for questioning in what could be
a murder case.

At the station Sergeant Beeney
said DS Magic and DCI Dirk were
waiting in interview room three.
Gammon turned to take Steve in
when Sergeant Beeney said Dirk had
told him that DI Gammon was not to
be present at the interview, and that
he was to take Mr Lineman in.

Steve looked at Gammon in
disbelief, and Gammon was furious.
The problem he had with Steve was
that he was emotional, and always
had been. If Dirk said the wrong

thing there was a chance he would deck him.

Gammon went to his office but just stared out of his window towards Losehill. What if Steve was guilty? How had he been so calm, other than when he broke down at the funeral? Was that because the enormity of what he had done had hit him?

Then Gammon started to think about the weeks before Jo had died and how she and Steve weren't getting on. Did all this make sense he thought.

After twenty minutes there was a hell of a commotion. Gammon shot out of his office and from the top of the stairs he could see Steve being man-handled down to the cells by DI Lee and DI Smarty. John got to the bottom of the stairs to be met by DCI

Dirk his shirt covered in blood his
eye cut and his nose bleeding.

"What happened Sir?"

"Come to my office now."

Gammon followed him back
upstairs and Dirk said to shut the
door.

"Your friend just struck me quite a
few times, DI Gammon."

"I'm sorry, Sir."

"Well he isn't. He was like a rabid
dog in there, and for that he will get
a custodial sentence when I make my
report. I will make sure of that."

"I understand your anger Sir, but
what if he apologised to you?"

"No Gammon, a man with a
temper like that could kill somebody.
In fact he probably did and we all
know who that is."

Gammon could feel anger welling
up inside him. That was a cheap shot
from Dirk.

THE CURE

"What made him kick off?"

"The questions I was asking him about the findings. That's all Gammon. Oh, and I do not want you going down to the holding cells or having any involvement in this case. Do I make myself clear? It's too close to home."

Gammon didn't answer. He just left Saul with blood dripping on his desk from his nose and cut eye. He knew he should have been present. He knew that Steve is like a bottle of pop at times waiting to go off.

Gammon ignored Dirk and decided to go to the burnt-out house to see if Wally had found anything. The drive to the burnt-out house was most unpleasant. He was just hoping they had got it wrong.

Wally had three big white tents and there was all the forensic team scurrying about. Wally was just coming out of the first tent and saw John.

"This isn't looking good for your mate John. The pipe that was slit has fingerprints on it. If they are Lineman's then he is bang to rights."

"Keep looking Wally. Steve wouldn't do that, I know he wouldn't. There has to be an explanation of something we are missing mate."

"I will know more tomorrow John. DCI Dirk wants a full report for the incident room by 9.00am."

Gammon left Wally feeling even more down than when he arrived. He knew if the fingerprints were Steve's he would possibly be convicted on that alone.

Gammon decided to see if Tracey was home and to keep her up to speed. John knocked on the lodge door. Tracey's car was outside.

"Hello John, you ok?"

Tracey's eyes were still bloodshot from all the crying yesterday.

"Do you want a coffee?"

"Yes please, strong black no sugar."

Tracey went in the kitchen to make the coffee and returned with a cup for both of them. On the coffee table she had photographs when Jo and her were kids.

"Tracey, I have bad news."

"Not more John, not sure I can cope."

"They have kept Steve down at Bixton station, they are questioning him about Jo and Leah Marie's deaths."

"What, are you serious?"

"Sorry, but yes. I have been told I am too close to Steve so cannot be involved in the case."

"Case, what bloody case? Steve wouldn't hurt his family, he loved them John."

"I know that. He was questioned by DCI Dirk when let his temper get the better of him and he hit the officer. DCI Dirk will press charges, which could mean a custodial sentence even without all this crap about him being involved in the fire."

"Why do they think he was involved with the fire?"

"The flexible pipe leading to the cooker had been slit. The problem is I have just been to see forensics, and they have found fingerprints on the pipe. I am praying they aren't Steve's."

THE CURE

"Didn't the fire destroy everything?"

"No, the pipe they showed me was almost ok. There are a few other things from just glancing round which were ok. The Fire Service also reported the use of barbecue lighter fuel."

"Oh, John no. I will never believe it was Steve."

"Me too Tracey, but I am on the outside looking in on this, and it isn't looking good for my mate."

Just then John's phone rang.

"Hi John, just want to say thank you for last night. Sorry I left but I have a lot to do with having yesterday off for the funeral."

"No problem, was lovely to see you. Do you fancy having a night out this week?"

"Oh, I will see John, the pub is quite tying. Speak soon," and Saron hung up.

Well that pretty much told me John thought.

"Look Tracey, I will share what I find out, but you mustn't share with anyone, and that includes Steve."

Gammon left Tracey possibly feeling worse than when he arrived, but he couldn't just leave her in the dark. It was lunch time, so he called at Beryl's Baps, one of his favourite places. He usually only had breakfast but decided he was hungry.

The place was quite full and John stood out somewhat in his suit, when most of the clientele were builders or truckers. He sat by the window and glanced at the menu.

A waitress arrived.

THE CURE

"What can I do you for?" she said. This made John chuckle even though he was feeling down about his mate.

"Can I have a Belly Buster Fish Finger sandwich, no salad, beer battered fries and a side of tartar sauce. Oh, and a strong black coffee please."

"Will mayonnaise do?" she said.

"Not a problem."

John smiled at her abruptness. She wasn't taking any prisoners. Did she mean mayonnaise with his coffee? Again it made him smile.

John didn't have to wait long when an enormous sandwich came out and enough fries to feed a school on the side. He had two slices of white bread cut about two inches thick. Inside each slice were eight beer battered fish fingers with cheese on top, which was a bit of a surprise.

He didn't order cheese and it never
mentioned it on the menu.

It took John almost half an hour to
eat the enormous sandwich and his
fries swilled down with his coffee.

He paid the waitress and gave her
a tip of two pounds which she smiled
at, showing an enormous gap in her
teeth.

John headed back to Bixton.
Sergeant Beeney said that DCI Dirk
had said when he got back he was to
go to his office. Here we go again
John thought.

He climbed the stairs and knocked
on DCI's door.

"Come in," he bellowed.

John felt like a naughty school boy
about to be chastised as he entered
Dirk's office.

"Sit down Gammon."

THE CURE

Gammon sat across from DCI Dirk and he could feel the anger rising up inside of him.

"Listen John, maybe I was being a bit over the top with regard to my attitude earlier. I am starting to get quite a bit of pressure from above with regard to these murders, and now we have the situation with your friend and the fire. I have to say John it is getting to me somewhat, and to cut possibly my best officer out of the loop on anything is not sensible. What I propose on the situation with your friend is you don't do any interviews, but I want you on the case helping to get to the truth. So, you will be in the incident room etc. I think that is fair to you."

"I appreciate that Sir. You know I will be professional."

"Any other way never crossed my mind John. I suggest we get a

meeting in the incident room at
9.30am when forensics should have
more on the fire."

"Ok Sir, thanks."

Gammon left the office thinking to
himself maybe just maybe this guy
he could work with.

It was almost 5.10pm when
Gammon could hear the other
officers going past his office on their
way home. Gammon shut down his
computer and called it a night.

He nipped into Bixton hoping to
get to the dry cleaners before they
shut at 6.00pm. He did and dropped
two suits off that he had been
meaning to get cleaned for some
time. He then headed to the Spinning
Jenny. To his surprise Sheba Filey
and Phil Sterndale were sitting at the
bar. Kev was looking studious
behind the bar reading the Racing

THE CURE

Post. Carol Lestar and her mum, Freda were having a bar meal by the fire. Before he could get a drink Carol shouted him over.

"John, Mum has something to say to you."

"John, I really can't thank you enough. Let me buy you a drink."

"Freda, I am buying you and Carol a drink. To see you looking so well, it's made my day."

"You are a lovely man, John Gammon, you really are."

Freda said she would have a half of Guinness and black, and Carol went for a double vodka and skinny coke as she called it.

John spoke with Sheba and Phil and took the drinks back to the girls, before returning to the bar and his pint of Pedigree.

"How are you keeping John?"

"Not bad Phil, thanks. What about you?"

"Well as you know I bought back the farm, so been busy getting cattle in. I am keeping the barns and will turn them into holiday lets. Let me buy you a drink John. I know we didn't hit it off, but you were only doing your job. Now me and Sheba are an item I would like to think we can get on."

"Seems fair to me Phil. I'll have a pint of Pedigree please."

Phil got John a drink and one for him and Sheba, then nipped to the toilet.

"Thanks John."

"What for?"

"Getting on with Phil, that means a lot to me."

"No problem, pleased you are happy Sheba."

THE CURE

It was now 7.00pm and Anouska took over the bar. Kev came and stood with John, Phil and Sheba at the bar.

"How many of those red dickie bows have you got, Kev?"

"Dozens Sheba."

"Really," and she laughed.

"What's so funny?"

"Just as long as I have known you, they have been a part of your attire behind the bar."

"I like to look smart when I am serving my customers, dear."

"And you always are Kev."

"Thank you, dear."

"So Phil, you are getting the old farm back on its feet I hear."

"Yes mate."

"Well I am pleased for you lad, good to hear somebody is doing well."

John was still drinking at 9.00pm when Phil and Sheba left. Carol and her mum had gone just after their meal so it only left Kev, four holiday makers that were now sitting by the fire and Anouska behind the bar.

"It is quiet night, Kevin," Anouska remarked in broken English.

"Yes, funny time of the year for the pub trade, Anouska."

"Well you two, going to love you and leave you, got a long day tomorrow."

John was pleased that Kev hadn't asked about Steve, maybe he didn't know.

"Goodnight."

"John, I will follow you out I want to ask you something."

Kev followed John onto the car park.

"What the hell happened with young Lineman, John?"

THE CURE

John told him the story but omitted that he might have been involved in the fire.

"Bloody hot head, you can't go around hitting policemen, John."

"Well certainly not a DCI, Kev."

"I heard they were holding him."

"Who told you?"

"A friend of Doreen's works for a cleaning company that does the station at nights, and she saw Steve in the holding cells."

"Oh, ok anyway mate might see you tomorrow."

"Ok drive safely, John."

The following day John arrived at the station with his fingers and toes crossed that whatever Wally had found didn't incriminate Steve further.

The incident room was full and DCI Dirk was taking the meeting.

"Ok everyone. I want to talk first about the fire which you are all aware of. I have Steve Lineman in the holding cells. DI Gammon is a close friend and I have asked him not to be part of any interviews of Mr Lineman. Ok, with that put to bed what have you got John?"

John Walvin came to the front.

"We found Mr Lineman's fingerprint on the split pipe. We also found his finger prints on some barbecue lighter fuel in one of the sheds that were untouched by the fire. We also found money in a hessian sack in the rafters of the shed. The money amounted to almost eighty five thousand pounds."

"Anything else, John?"

"No that's it."

"Yes, DI Scooper?"

"I did what you asked Sir and checked his bank account. He hadn't withdrawn any money and certainly not to that amount. The odd thing is about eight months ago he took out two individual life insurance policies on his and Jo's lives that would pay out three hundred thousand pounds!"

"I think we have enough there to re-interview Mr Lineman under caution. DI Scooper and myself will do this once his solicitor arrives."

"Now the murders that are stacking up, where are we on these DI Gammon?"

Gammon went to the front.

"Ok Sir, the victims," and he pointed to a photograph of Jessie Toppin of Manor Hill Farm, Hittington.

"The second victim is Maga Wuxi a Chinese student. Victim three is Helen Firm. All the victims had small traces of what we all know as bleach."

"We have five possible suspects; Mark Block a junior doctor at Micklock hospital, boyfriend of Jessie. Whilst he would have the knowledge my feelings are he saves people not kills them."

"Suspect two; Andrew Firm, husband of victim three Helen Firm, not a nice guy they were all but split."

"Suspect three; David Sowers, he came on our radar because of a thirty years sentence for administrating bleach, just like our killer."

"Suspect four; Jackie Bush Sowers, wife at the time that David Sowers was convicted. It was thought at the time they were in it together, but he took the fall."

"Suspect five; Andrew Gilbon, our strongest suspect to date, Gilbon's DNA was found on Maga Wuxi. We staked out Gilbon's house and he brought a friend of Helen Firm, Jane Sharpe to his house. I heard her screaming and found him cowering in corner with two injuries from a stiletto heel. DI Lee and DS Magic interviewed Gilbon, so if DI Lee would like to explain his findings."

DI Lee came to the front.

"We found Andrew Gilbon very sure of himself, he had time to work out his story. On the Jane Sharpe issue, he said she had gone willingly to his home. He also said she had made the first move, but for some reason flipped out and started attacking him. That's when DI Gammon came on the scene. Jane Sharpe doesn't want to press charges. He also said it was a misunderstanding, and so we have little choice but to drop this. On the DNA found on Maga Wuxi, he said that Maga had been in a pub where he had been. She dropped her handbag and he said he picked it up. That is possibly why his DNA was on it. He said he didn't know Maga but he had seen her on the campus, as he works as a janitor at the same university. I think there is more to this guy than we are seeing."

"So, what do you recommend DI Lee?"

"I would do a sting operation."

DI Scooper put her hand up.

"I will volunteer, Sir."

"Ok, DI Scooper thank you. Speak with DI Lee after the meeting and let's see what we can do here."

"Ok, what about the others? Any we can discount?" said DCI Dirk.

"Yes Sir, Jackie Bush-Sowers. She now lives in Newcastle and our sources tell us she is terminally ill."

"Ok, let's take her off the list. What about her husband?"

THE CURE

"Well with his past record of using bleach we should keep a close eye on him."

"Right, I want twenty four hour surveillance on him, the beat lads can do that. Magic sort with Sergeant Beeney."

"Yes, Sir."

"So that leaves Block and Firm, thoughts please team?"

"Yes, Smarty."

"I think DI Gammon is correct, Block is a doctor saving lives not taking them."

"Ok, do we all agree?"

Everybody said yes.

"Ok, let's strike him off. That leaves Firm, and my thoughts are he isn't a nice guy, but wasting resources on him in my opinion would be futile. What do we all think?"

Eighty percent agreed with DCI
Dirk.

"Ok, strike him off. So that leaves
Gilbon and the sting operation.

DS Magic is sorting the beat lads
for David Sower. DI Lee you are
sorting the sting operation on Gilbon
with DI Scooper. Keep me
informed," and he strode out of the
room like a peacock.

THE CURE

CHAPTER THREE

Gammon kept his thoughts to himself, but he pretty much knew that Steve would be charged today. He could not help his best mate. The only thing he could do was to dig around and ask questions which hopefully might turn something up. He also decided to look into Steve and Jo's bank accounts. He knew he would be bombed out of the force if he was caught. Steve had been a great mate for John even going to Ireland to see Saron after his accident. He felt he owed him and there was only John could help him.

At 5.00pm John decided to go and see Tracey Rodgers to see if she could help with Steve. John arrived at the lodge and Tracey opened the door.

"Blimey, I am honoured to see you again. Come in I'll pour us a wine."

"I don't have good news Tracey, there were Steve's fingerprints on the pipe. They also found a stash of money in one of the outbuildings."

Tracey's face went white.

"Are you ok?"

"What are you telling me, John?"

"I am quite sure DCI Dirk will charge Steve over the deaths of Jo and Leah Marie. I expected it today, but it hadn't happened by the time I left. I am pretty sure DCI Dirk thinks he will get the CPS to accept he has a case, and there is nothing I can do."

"So, how can I help?"

"What do you know about Jo?"

"Well, we didn't really get on when we were younger, and then she moved away. I remember Dad came home from work one night, and I heard him tell Mum that a guy from work had been at a pole dancing club. He said our Jo worked there but mother was having none of it, John."

"Did you see any strangers hanging round the house lately?"

"Not really. No hang on a minute, I did see Jo talking to two really big guys. One had one of those fighting dogs. I could hear our Jo's voice, it was quite raised."

"Did you hear what she said?"

"Well I was rushing, but I think she said tell him to stay in his Derby flea pit. I'm not bothered anymore."

"What do you think that meant then, Tracey?"

"Not got a clue, our Jo was always a private person."

"You didn't by any chance see a vehicle, did you?"

"Yes, as I was leaving this white van almost run me off the road."

"Registration number?"

"It was a 61 plate Ford Transit, and it had blue writing on the side and back doors, which I think said Billgate Butchers, and an address that ended in Derby."

"Ok thanks Tracey, and for the drink."

"You not stopping?"

"No, sorry got a lot on tonight."

"Maybe another night then?"

"Yeah, maybe," and John left.

He decided to call at the Spinning Jenny for one of Doreen's mixed grills. The pub was quite full. It was now 7.40pm. Kev, Anouska and Joni were behind the bar.

"Busy night, Kev," he said as he fought his way to order a pint.

"Yeah, it's Hittington Darts and Dominos presentation night."

THE CURE

"Well I was going to have one of Doreen's mixed grills."

"Not tonight mate, she is busy with the buffet, and even you could not get a mixed grill from her tonight."

John thought he would just have the one go. He pulled away from the bar and at the far side were Sheba and Phil, Bob and Cheryl, Jack and Shelley and Carol Lestar so he wandered over.

"Now then old lad, what about young Lineman? I hear they have him at Bixton."

"Yes Jack, they do."

"I can't believe it if it's true?"

"If what's true, Cheryl?"

They are saying he did her in for the insurance money, Carol. Well people do the oddest things."

"Look to put you all straight, Steve hasn't been charged with anything. They are looking at all possibilities."

"Well I don't believe it John, not Steve. He loved Jo and that little girl."

"It would be more believable if it had been those two idiots that came in here a bit back looking for Jo's place. They stopped at Jeanette's place in Dilley Dale."

"Did they, Phil? Thanks."

John drank his pint in one and made his excuses and left. He drove down to Dilley Dale Ices hoping Jeanette was in.

Lucky for John she was, and she answered the door almost immediately.

"You ok John?"

"I need your help Jeanette. If I can come in?"

THE CURE

She still lived in the big farm house tending to her poorly mother, making ice cream and running the holiday lets.

John told her the situation with Steve knowing he could trust her.

"Phil Sterndale met a couple of shady characters in the Spinning Jenny who were looking for Jo's place. I know they stayed here."

"I said I didn't know her because they looked evil. They wanted one of them fighting dogs to stay in the room with them, but I said no so it slept in their van."

"You say van?"

"Yes, a white Transit with a butcher's name on it. I took the number plate because I was concerned. They were big men, John. Both had shaven heads and one had a rose tattoo on his neck."

"Would you say the tattoo was new or old?"

"No definitely old John, it was quite faded."

John felt like kissing Jeanette. It was what he was looking for. He wrote down the number of the vehicle and the address Jeanette had scribbled down for him. He really felt he was making progress.

"I was so sorry the wedding got called off, John. How is Saron with you now?"

"I took her to Jo and Leah Marie's funerals."

"I felt so bad John, I couldn't make it. Mum was really poorly and I couldn't leave her, she is getting worse."

"Sorry to hear that Jeanette. I'm sure Steve would understand but I guess he has so much on his plate it would be the least of his troubles.

THE CURE

Anyway, the information you gave me may help."

"John, I hope you don't think I am breaking a confidence, but Jo had been a pole dancer not an air hostess. She told me ages ago when we first met. I wonder if that has anything to do with it. Do they think its murder?"

"Yes, they do, but you must not say anything please."

"Of course I won't, John, how dreadful, isn't it?"

"John please don't think I am being funny, but I have to get Mum her Horlicks, and get her settled down for the night."

"Not a problem, thanks for your help."

John gave Jeanette a peck on the cheek then headed home.

Once back at the cottage he poured himself a generous measure of Jameson's and sat down and wrote down his thoughts.

'Two men, one with a faded rose tattoo on his neck

Fighting dog

Butchers van

Address: Billgate Butchers, Wright Road, Lychen Estate, Derby.'

He knew what his first job was going to be in the morning at work. Look up anybody with a neck tattoo in the National Police Database.

The following morning John wanted to get into work early to look on the data base before DCI Dirk arrived. He knew this was all risky, but he had to do it.

Gammon arrived and had a quick word with Sergeant Beeney then headed to his office. He sat at his computer to look for tattoo man on the data base.

He had been looking only five minutes when his door opened. It was DCI Dirk.

"Early today Gammon?"

"Yes Sir, couldn't sleep."

Dirk made his way basically to look at what Gammon was looking at, and just by luck DI Lee appeared. He asked if he could have a minute of DCI Dirk's time. Dirk turned around and as he was leaving he turned to Gammon.

"Just to let you know, I am charging Steve Lineman with arson which lead to the death of Jo Wickets and Leah Marie."

John needed to find some evidence and quick.

Gammon carried on looking. He had been at it almost four hours when he got something although the

guy wasn't a big guy, His name was
Leroy Gabble. It said he was from
Derby and he had a record of
violence and one for threatening
behaviour with a gun which he got
four years for. It said he had walked
into Bambi's nightclub went up to
one of the bouncers and threatened
to blow his head off. A civilian who
was a black belt wrestled him to the
ground. After Gabble was convicted
and sent down the civilian, Nick
White, was found dead in a Derby
park with his throat cut. It was
widely believed that his younger
brother, Piers Gabble, carried out the
crime, but nothing could be proved
because nobody would come
forward and testify.

Last known address of the two
brothers said Sussex. Gammon put in
the butcher's shop that was on the
van and confirmed it was Billgate

THE CURE

Butchers. John decided to slip out and pay the shop a visit.

Gammon arrived at the butcher's shop on Wright Road, Lychen Estate. Gammon went in the shop and a small guy came out. The first thing that hit him was the state of the guy, he had a black eye and a huge lump on his head.

Gammon went straight for it and showed his warrant card.

"How can I help you, DI Gammon?"

"We have had a report about your van being driven recklessly in the Peak District about ten days ago. Would you have been driving?"

The butcher hesitated, "Possibly."

"Can I ask you what business you had in the Peak District Mr?"

"Simon Billgate, please call me Simon."

"Simon, why I don't believe you were driving? How did you get your injuries?"

"Come into the back. I will make us a drink and I want to tell you something. Billgate made their drinks and just as he was about to talk there was somebody shouting his name in the shop. Billgate gestured to Gammon stay in the back, but pointed to his ear as if to say listen.

"Hey Simple Simon, how are you bro?"

Gammon could hear Billgate say ok.

"So now you have had a little attention from me and my bro you will be a good boy. Sell some sweeties to the locals, you know like selling a pork pie, and some magic dust to the kids. You do this.."

THE CURE

Gammon decided he had heard enough, then the name stopped him in his tracks.

The voice finished off his sentence, "... and Mr Lund will be pleased."

"Ok, ok, I will sell to the kids, just let me make a living please."

"Let's see, we will be back, might need that van again anyway."

They left and Simon Billgate came back into the back.

"You weren't driving that van, were you?"

"No Mr Gammon. Look I will tell you everything, but you can't involve me, or they will kill me."

"Who will kill you, Simon?"

"Leroy and Piers Gabble."

"Who do they work for?"

"The scum work for Brian Lund, they say he is untouchable, Mr Gammon."

Gammon was thinking you aren't wrong there.

"So, you have to sell drugs for these men who work for Brian Lund. Look Simon, I will work something out, but it may mean you get a suspended sentence on the drugs. I will come back and see you very soon."

Gammon left the butchers shop and drove back to share his knowledge with DCI Dirk. He was feeling quite good he had something on Lund, and he possibly had the people responsible for Jo and Leah Marie's death. The day could not get any better.

Gammon arrived at the station the desk Sergeant collared him as soon as he arrived.

THE CURE

"DCI Dirk wants you in his office, Sir."

"Ok, Sergeant Beeney."

Gammon grabbed a quick coffee and knocked on DCI Dirk's door.

"Come in," came the booming voice.

"Morning Sir."

"Yes, a bloody good morning to you."

Gammon didn't like the tone in DCI Dirk's voice.

"As you are aware, I have today charged Steve Lineman with the arson attack at his home which led to the deaths of Jo Wickets and Leah Marie."

"I have something on that Sir."

"Hold it there, Gammon. What did I say to you?"

"You said you didn't want me involved in the interviews or possible charging of Mr Lineman because he was a close friend of mine."

"Correct, and I told you that I was about to charge Lineman. Is that correct?"

"Look Sir, with the greatest respect, where is this going?"

"I'll tell you where it's going. I am seconding you to Staffordshire Police until Lineman's trial is over."

"What?"

"I can't have you running around the country on a case that is closed until the trial, when we have a serial killer at large. I have had a call from the Assistant Chief Commissioner. He has told me that you are to leave Brian Lund alone. He is an important snout in the fight against crime in the Derbyshire area."

"This is bollocks. So Steve Lineman takes the fall for a crime he didn't commit. Lund and his evil buddies walk away free. I get moved to some rural police force, and all because Lund has some kind of connection high up in the police force. Do you think that's right?"

"It doesn't matter what I think Gammon, and you will address me as Sir. Am I clear?"

Gammon knew he was overstepping the mark, and thinking about it, Staffordshire Police might be a good move. Away from prying eyes he could work on Steve's case.

"When do you want me to leave for Staffordshire?"

"Leave Bixton immediately, Gammon. You are reporting to DCI Douglas Oldfield in Stoke on Trent in the morning. I will be in touch. Clear your desk."

Gammon was fuming but still thought this might help Steve. Steve had been taken to Leicester. He wanted to visit him, but knowing the cons, if they got a whiff Steve's best mate was a copper it could be hell for him. It won't be good if they think he has killed a child John thought. John needed a mate so headed for Kev and the Spinning Jenny.

It was 4.10pm. In the bar area were quite a few walkers dotted about. Kev was down the cellar so John waited at the bar. Eventually he came up from cellar and closed the trap door behind the bar.

"Hello John, you're early lad."

"Yeah, a few things happened today."

"Well I best get you a pint and you can tell your Uncle Kev all about it."

Kev smiled as he went down the bar to the Pedigree pimp for John's pint.

"So why the glum look?"

THE CURE

"My DCI charged Steve today Kev, with arson that led to the deaths of Jo and Leah Marie."

"Oh, that is dreadful lad. I know Steve can be a bit hot headed at times, but he has a heart of gold."

"Well, I want to ask a favour of you mate. I wasn't allowed to see Steve while he was at Bixton. If I go to see him in Leicester and word gets out I am a copper it will be horrendous for him inside. Could you or Doreen get a visiting order and see him?"

"Of course, lad."

"Please explain the situation. Tell him I am looking into this, and not to give up."

"Will do mate, it will give him hope."

"It's a long story Kev, but I have been transferred to Staffordshire,

well Stoke on Trent actually, until
Steve's case his heard."

"Why John?"

"Well, my superiors found out I
was digging for answers, and for
some reason they don't want me to.
At first I was fuming, but thinking
about it, this might work in my
favour. I can carry on digging away
from the eyes of my DCI."

"Well the man is an idiot. You are
the best copper Bixton ever had, and
we would be in a right pickle if it
hadn't been for you in the last few
years, John."

"Thanks Kev, good of you to say.
Obviously everything I tell you is in
confidence."

Kev peered over his glasses as
much to say he should know he
won't breathe a word.

"Can I order a Doreen mixed grill
to go, mate? Best get an early night

THE CURE

if I am to go to Stoke in the morning."

"Sure, she will do that for you lad."

John ordered another pint then waited for his mixed grill which the kitchen help brought out in a plate covered in tin foil.

"Right mate, I'm off," John said as he paid the bill.

"Ok mate, see you soon, good luck."

John left with his mixed grill and drove as quick as he could to the cottage. Nobody could touch Doreen's mixed grill, not even John's mum when she was alive.

He had a big piece of steak, two Cumberland sausages, a lamb chop, a large gammon, two slices of streaky bacon, scrambled eggs with cream and mustard; simply unbelievable. Then there was liver, black pudding, a stack of onion rings, fried tomato, beans and Doreen's home-made Welsh mash with horseradish and cranberry juice. This meal was to die for.

John cleared his plate and sat for a minute feeling like his tummy was going to burst.

He showered then set his alarm for 6.30am. The drive to Stoke was about fifty minutes and he didn't want to be late on his first day.

The following morning John made it to Stoke Police Station which was quite a grand Victorian building. The traffic on the way meant John took almost one hour, but that was fine as it was only 8.10am.

Gammon went straight to the front desk to introduce himself.

THE CURE

"Pleased to meet you Sir, Sergeant Musgrave."

"Likewise, Sergeant."

"We have an office ready for you Sir. DCI Oldfield will be along about 9.00am."

Sergeant Musgrave showed John to his office. It was quite plush and certainly put his Bixton office to shame. The only thing wrong was the view; he now had a high rise set of flats to look at instead of Losehill but hey he thought, you can't have everything.

It was 9.10am when DCI Oldfield came into his office. Oldfield was in his late fifties with quite a head of white hair for his age. He was about six feet tall John thought.

Oldfield shook John's hand.

"Very pleased to have you on the stations team, John. I have heard a lot about you. You are a man that

gets results, and I like that I think
they call it old policing, don't they?"

"I guess so, Sir."

"I have set a meeting in ten
minutes in the incident room which
is on the second floor; left at the top
of the stairs, and go right to the end,
up the next flight of stairs, turn left
and follow your nose John. It's for
you to meet your new colleagues and
a chance to take a look at a case we
are working on."

"Ok Sir, that will be great."

Gammon left his laptop and
headed for the stairs. He found the
incident room. As he walked in the
whole room clapped, which John felt
a bit embarrassed about. A few
seconds later DCI Oldfield came in
and went straight to the front calling
John to follow him.

"Ok everybody, judging by the
clapping I heard coming up the stairs

you sussed out this is DI John Gammon from Bixton Police in Derbyshire. Pretty good set of detectives eh John," and he laughed.

"I would like you to stand up one at a time say your rank and name please. Let's start now."

A young woman in her late twenties stood up. "

"Amy Bogdan, Detective Sergeant."

"Jim Kelly, Detective Inspector."

"Harry Looks, Detective Inspector."

"Sarah Stone, Detective Inspector, Karen Bools, Detective Sergeant."

"Jim Clark, Detective Sergeant."

"Astra Coogan, Detective Inspector."

"Andrew Mason, Detective Sergeant."

"John Brooky, Detective Inspector."

"Ok thank you."

"DI Gammon, we work in pairs mainly here in Stoke, so you will be working with Detective Sergeant Karen Bools. Ok, take a seat John. Let's run through our current case."

"Jim, would you like to take us through this case please."

Jim Clark came to the front. He was about five feet ten. He looked physically fit and John thought he was maybe fifty eight, although he did look younger.

"Yes, the case as it stands has been a long case, almost a year now. Two brothers came to our attention. They own two night clubs; one in Hanley, The Magic Trip, and one in Burslem called Fried Onions. Early in 2017 two girls were found a week apart in an alleyway. They had taken Fizz pills, as they call them round here. Apparently, they give you a quick hit

THE CURE

like heroin, but are not as addictive. Both girls had been in the Magic Trip in Hanley on two different Saturdays one week apart."

"A snout of DS Bools told her that the brothers made these pills, but he didn't know where, and they sold them in their club. The catch here is they don't actual sell themselves. They have kids of about eighteen that they bring in from neighbouring counties. These are generally Polish or Latvian. They don't use the same sellers each time therefore if they get caught, it's a fine and a slap on the wrist which covertly the brothers pay. We have suspicion that they are branching out, and we believe they are headed in your direction DI Gammon, to Derby. There isn't a lot more to add, Sir."

"Ok, DI Gammon you will be working with DS Karen Bools while

you are on loan to us. Good to have
you onboard."

They all left except DS Bools.

"DS Bools, Sir," she said thrusting
out her hand.

Bools was about five feet seven,
slim with a good figure. She was
quite pretty with dark hair, a bit like
the actress Demi Moor when she was
in 'Ghost' the film he thought.

"Please to meet you DS Bools. Do
you mind if I call you Karen?"

"No Sir."

"Look when it's just us two, it's
John."

"Oh, ok John."

"Can I have a chat with your snout
Karen?"

"I'll see if he will see us."

Karen phoned a number in her
mobile. After a few minutes she said
Jimmy Brimble, her snout, would

meet us at the canal side café at Frog Wharf.

"It's outside Stoke, but he feels safer away from the area."

"Understand Karen, I think I may have passed that wharf on the way here."

"Ok let's go and see him."

It was a good forty minutes to the Wharf and they chatted about incidental things in the car. The Wharf Café was in an old maintenance /repair shed. It was quite pleasant, and John ordered a strong coffee and water for DS Bools. They waited almost half an hour and were about to leave when Brimble arrived.

Brimble was a strange looking character he was about five feet eight with a jacket that looked like it was straight from the charity shop, and trousers that were quite short. He had a green hoodie under the suit jacket. He was unshaven and his teeth were not in the best condition.

"Sit down Jimmy, would you like a drink?"

"Please coffee, white, four sugars. Can I have a meat pie as well? I've not eaten for two days."

Bools said yes and went off to get Jimmy's order.

"So, Mr Brimble, I'm DI John Gammon."

"I know who you are, everyone knows who you are."

"Really?"

"Yeah, you had a run in with Brian Lund and his mob didn't you? Your brother shot his twin brother."

This man seemed highly informed.

"Word is, you have crossed Brian again. Not a wise move, Mr Gammon."

THE CURE

Bools came back with a meat pie, a sandwich and a drink for Brimble. He set about the pie and sandwich like a man that hadn't eaten for some time. It was quite disgusting to watch Gammon thought.

Bools and Gammon let Brimble finish and then Gammon asked him some questions.

"So, you know Mr Lund then Jimmy?"

"Maybe, why?"

"Well as you know, I have history with the man."

"Yeah, but he is protected, isn't he?"

"Protected, what from the law?"

"That's what they say on the streets."

"So, does Mr Lund have any input in the running of the Magic Trip club in Hanley and the Fried Onion club in Burslem?"

Jimmy laughed showing his inadequate dental hygiene.

"What is so funny?" Karen Bools said.

"Just your man here. Brian Lund owns and runs those clubs."

"I thought the two brothers owned and ran those clubs."

"They run them and their names are over the door, but only one man runs Stoke Mr Gammon, and that's Mr Lund."

"So, what do you know about the two girls found a week apart with drugs inside them."

"It's called Fizz, the kids take it at the clubs."

"Where is it supplied from?"

"Nobody knows, but my guess Lund has it manufactured somewhere maybe in Derby."

Gammon had heard enough.

THE CURE

"Ok Jimmy, if there is anything else I will be in touch."

"Only let DS Bools contact me. If I am ever found to be a snout Mr Gammon, then I am a dead man walking."

"I understand Jimmy, I know how it works."

"Come on DS Bools, let's make a move. Thanks again Jimmy."

Brimble smiled at Gammon which made John's stomach churn. What a mess he thought.

"Is he reliable, Karen?"

"Pretty much, he hasn't let me down, although he has got a drug habit."

"I guessed that, looking at his skin and his teeth, Karen."

It was 5.10pm so John dropped Karen off at the station and made his way back to the Spinning Jenny. On the way he phoned Dave Smarty.

"Hey John, how are you mate?"

"Been better, Dave."

"Rum do, sending our best officer to Stoke just because his mate has been charged for a crime."

"A crime he didn't commit, and I will prove it Dave."

"Sorry John, I didn't mean anything. If he is a mate of yours he will be a sound bloke I'm sure."

"He has been set up mate, I'm sure. I intend to prove it, and while I am in Stoke, to some degree they have done me a favour, I can investigate, and they don't know. How are things in Bixton?"

"We have had another body turn up, John. I am assuming it will be our serial killer, but until John Walvin reports his findings in the morning we can't be sure."

THE CURE

"Do you have a name?"

"Yes mate. A lady was out running and saw the girl's leg sticking from under a bush. She knew her, and said her name was Mandy Bellow from Ibley. Her dad is ex Sergeant Walt Bellow, formerly at Bixton Police Station. He retired on ill health grounds apparently about fourteen years back."

"I don't know him Dave, before my time at Bixton. Who broke the news?"

"DCI Dirk and DS Magic, I believe."

"Sad mate, any correspondence from our killer?"

"Nothing yet John, but maybe he will contact you?"

"Ok, will let you know mate. Just on my way home now."

"Let me know nearer the weekend and we can nip for a beer, mate."

"Will do Dave, keep me up to speed."

John rang off as he pulled in the car park of the Spinning Jenny.

Doreen was just off walking the dogs.

"Hear you are working in Stoke John, is it permanent?"

"No Doreen, only until Steve's case is heard."

"Well if it's any consolation, none of the locals think the lad did it John."

"I know Doreen, it's just proving it now."

"I'm sure you will find a way, John," and she left with the dog pulling her along the car park.

Anouska was on the bar with no sign of Kev.

"Hello handsome."

John smiled.

THE CURE

"Evening Anouska, no Kev tonight?"

"No, he has got the man flu, as they call it over here."

John laughed, "Oh, right."

"So how is John? I heard you leave for Stoke on Trent, yet you are back?"

"I am travelling Anouska, and it will only be for a few months, just helping the Stoke force out."

John wasn't going to go into the ins and outs of the reason for his secondment.

"What would you like to drink John, or have you just come to admire me?"

He could certainly do that he thought. She was dressed in yellow hot pants with a brown see-through blouse, most delightful he thought. He had noticed quite a few village lads in their late teens had started

coming to the pub, and it was only
Anouska that was the pull. Kev was
a wily old bird, he knew what he was
doing.

John just had two pints then drove
home. He wanted to take a look at
his laptop to see if he could find
anything else out for Steve.

He entered the cottage and it was
freezing. He went straight to the
boiler and the flame had blown out.
He played about with it and
eventually got it to light so then he
had hot water and heat. John then put
in the oven a home–made Lasagne
from the freezer that Phyllis the
cleaner had made for him.

He kept his coat on while the
rooms heated up. John sat with his
laptop. He had purposely left the
police data base open from earlier.
He knew that if he got caught using

it away from the station it would be instant dismissal.

John put in the name of the drug, Fizz, because he was sure somehow that Lund was manufacturing it. But what he didn't know was Jo's involvement, and what he needed to do was make the tie up, then maybe there would be a motive.

John grabbed his lasagne, covered it with salad cream and a couple of slices of crust bread, then went back to his computer.

John opened Jo's bank account. There were monthly transactions for the last four years. The amounts varied, the least being three and half years ago when in March and April she received seven thousand pounds. Nearly all the monies credited to her account were for eleven thousand pounds and as much as eighteen thousand pounds. In the last two

months of December and January
there was no money put in.

John knew he was onto something.
The monies were deposited by a
company called Acclimatised Inc.

John put the name of the company
into company's house web site and
bingo. The directors of the company
were; Company Secretary Mr Brian
Lund, Operations Director Philip
Gregg, and Financial Director Maria
Snood.

John could feel his heart racing.
How come nobody had picked up on
this, or was Steve the fall guy for the
untouchable Lund?

He put the name of the Operations
Director, Philip Gregg. It gave a
London address, 18 Murcle Flats,
Greenwich, a director for six years.
Then John put in Maria Snood; again
another London address, Malvern
House, Chelsea. She has been a

director for four and a half years. It also said Gregg was owner and Managing Director of Prestige Cars London Limited. But the interesting one was Marie Snood, who was the Managing Director of Debauched, a Gentlemen's Club in Soho. Now the pieces were fitting together. Jo had told Jeanette she had been a pole dancer in London, and her house was left to her by an auntie. John decided this was too hot to wait until the weekend. He phoned Karen Bools to say he had come down with the flu and he wouldn't be at Stoke tomorrow. He felt bad having only done one day, but he needed to get to London and at least see Marie Snood.

John closed his laptop, rinsed his plate and cup and headed for bed. He set his alarm for 5.30am to get down to London. He was going to visit

Acclimatised Inc somehow. He wasn't sure how he would play this, but he wanted to get in and look round first.

Gammon pulled up at the company which was in Lewisham. The building was very impressive, and John thought it was probably forty thousand square feet in total.

Gammon parked and went into reception. Two young girls were on reception, so John took a chance and asked for Marie Snood and he showed her his warrant card

"Just let me check, she had a customer in with her."

"Miss Snood, I have a police officer wishing to talk with you."

The girl came off the phone and told John to enter his name on the H&S computer and it would print a badge, once he passed the five health and safety questions.

This was all very plush Gammon thought. He finished his questions and it printed his name badge out. As Gammon turned round he heard a lady say, "Mr Gammon come with me," then a quite loud guffaw.

"John boy, how nice to see you."

Gammon knew that voice straight away it was Lund. Lund was much thinner than when John had last seen him, and he was smartly dressed. Gammon scowled at him. That was the slice of luck he needed now he knew Lund was connected.

Gammon left Lund smirking as he followed Snood into her office. The office was also plush. All down the corridor he had noticed pictures of swimwear. Snood's office was immaculate with white carpets and stainless-steel glass tables with three

Chesterfield leather suites. The room
was massive. In one corner was a
rowing machine and an exercise
bike.

"So, Mr Gammon, how can I help
you?"

Marie Snood looked late forties
with shoulder length, blonde hair.
She was a bit heavy on the make-up
but had a good dress sense to go with
an excellent figure.

"Well I was hoping you could help
me."

"I see you are from the Derbyshire
police force."

"Yes, to be honest with you this
matter I would not normally get
involved with, but my DCI asked me
to have a chat."

"Well, we are investigating a fatal
accident that is looking increasingly
like an arson attack."

THE CURE

"So, what does that have to do with me and my company?"

Gammon didn't want to show his hand too much at this stage.

"Do you know this girl, Miss Snood?"

Gammon took out a picture he had of Jo from Pritwich sheep racing. It was a good picture of Jo, so if this woman would know her straight away. Snood looked for a few seconds then gave John the picture back and simply said, "No, why would I?"

"Well it was known that she lived in London. Somebody mentioned she had done some modelling work for some travel companies, you know like eighteen to thirty holidays, so we looked it up and she had your company sponsored bikini's etc. I realise it is a long shot Miss Snood."

"Not a problem Mr Gammon, but we tend to sponsor these things from our marketing team, and the travel people would have used a model agency I guess."

"Ok, Miss Snood thank you for the time. As I say it was a long shot."

Gammon was pretty sure that Snood knew Jo and he thought it funny she never mentioned Lund to him.

Next port of call was the gentleman's club in Soho. Gammon left his car on the outskirts and got the tube in. He decided to make out he was a client so he paid on the door.

The guy said, "There's no touching of the girls, but if you want you can pay extra and could have a private dance."

That was John's best chance he thought. He told the guy he liked a

THE CURE

girl in her thirties that way he thought they might remember Jo.

He was shown to a corridor and a room which was quite dimly lit but very clean with nice furniture. A woman came in and started gyrating in front of John. Gammon gestured with his finger to his mouth so she would understand not to scream or shout. Then he showed his warrant card and told her to sit in the chair opposite. He pulled out the picture of Jo and immediately the girl said, "Wickets, how do you know her?"

"I am afraid she and her daughter have been killed in a fire."

"Oh dear, lovely girl Jo, she set me on. When I came she was like the manager looking after the girls. I worked one weekend and when she came in she had a black eye. She said she was leaving. She wouldn't say where to."

"Why do you think that was?"

"Look, it's not for me to say but I think she got involved somehow with the owner and something to do with drugs, well that's what everyone reckoned."

"So, she was a drug user?"

"No, I don't think she was. She was just like a middleman or in this case middle woman. Where did she go to then Mr Gammon?"

"If you don't mind, I would prefer not to say. I would also appreciate you keep our chat to yourself," and John gave the girl a hundred pounds.

"Not a problem, Mr Gammon. I wish all the punters were like you."

Gammon thanked her and left.

He now decided to go and see where Snood lived. He found the address and walked down the tree lined road. At the end was Malvern

THE CURE

House, a massive imposing building, which must have been worth upwards of four million he thought.

With all the information Gammon decided to get back to Derbyshire. He was going to go and see DCI Dirk in the morning to get him to look at the information he had. He was convinced that somebody other than Steve had done the deed. He thought Dirk would not be happy with him, but he wasn't bothered. What mattered was getting Steve off and out of prison.

CHAPTER FOUR

The following day Gammon walked into Bixton police station. Sergeant Beeney said he had just been thinking about DI Gammon as a small parcel had arrived for DCI Dirk. On the back it said your officer Gammon and a smiley face.

"Is DCI Dirk in then?"

"Yes Sir, he comes in for eight now that you are in Stoke."

Gammon climbed the stairs and knocked on Dirk's door.

"Come in," he bellowed.

Gammon walked through the door.

"I have just called Stoke on Trent to talk to you. They said you are off with the flu?"

"Sir, I have something for you."

"Just hold it there, John."

THE CURE

Dirk slid a tape from out of a jiffy bag and placed it in his video machine.

The picture cleared and it was John with the girl gyrating in front of him in a dimly lit room. It had the date and the time on it.

"Did the flu get better John? You look ok to me and that video from yesterday looked like you were having a good time?"

Whoever sent the tape had only shown the recording at the beginning not all of the tape. It did show when he entered the club where he was paying to have a private dance with one of the girls.

"Sir, I can explain."

"John, do you know how this looks? You do know if I was to pass this on there would be a fair chance you would be out of a job."

"Just hear me out, Sir."

John explained why he was down in London what he had found out about Jo.

Dirk listened.

"Look John, you need to know this. When they asked me to take this position I had already applied for a job in the North East. My wife is from up there and she wanted to go back. They told me that this would be for six months as they were considering you for the position. But they had concerns that you could be a maverick and you had stood on some important toes in MI5 and MI6. They had to be sure you would leave that alone. They didn't tell me what it was about, but I just know that was their concern."

"So John whilst I sympathise with what you have found out, I also can't jeopardise my career. I suggest you go back to Stoke until this is over.

THE CURE

Then come back here and get on with your life. I will destroy this tape and will never mention this conversation to anybody."

John knew DCI Dirk was just trying to be right with him, so he played a long with his summary. It was almost lunch time, so John called in for his lunch at the Spinning Jenny and to see if Kev had been to see Steve in prison.

Kev pulled him a pint and they sat talking.

"Well first things first. I thought you were in Stoke, and unless I am mistaken this pub is in Derbyshire," and he laughed.

"It's a long story, I will tell you about when I have more time."

"Did you go to see Steve?"

"I did mate."

"How is he, Kev?"

"Very down mate, which is understandable. I told him you couldn't go because of you being the police. He said he understood but word was already out that you were best mates. Apparently two blokes got to him. They probably picked on the wrong guy with Steve; one is in hospital and the other one was badly beaten. Steve has a couple of black eyes, swollen lips and his knuckles were quite knocked about, so they have put him in solitary confinement for now."

"How are you doing with your investigation?"

"Ok mate, I think I am onto something. I don't think Steve is going to like it, but my gut feeling is Jo was involved in the high end of the drug market with some unsavoury characters. The house and the wealth looks like it may have been a front, Kev. But don't say anything to Steve."

"Did you tell him I was looking into it?"

"I did, John."

"What did he say?"

"He just said tell him to hurry up."

"I'm not sure what to do. I know a good private eye from my days in London. I am thinking about getting him involved, and if I have to I will send the evidence to the CPS and see if we can get Steve freed."

"Good luck with that lad."

"When are you going to see him again?"

"Hopefully next Monday."

"Let him know I am making progress, but don't say anything about the drugs and Jo please."

"No problem, mate. You having another?"

"No going home mate, I am goosed with all this chasing about."

John got back home and decided to again use the police data base. He knew he was running a great risk, but in his eyes it would be worth it. While he was looking at certain things he remembered a colleague in London that they called Anorak. Sergeant Tissler was an absolute wizard at breaking into people's bank accounts to see transactions. It was like an unwritten law he could get into anything, but only did it for the police. John wondered if he could get into Brian Lund's accounts.

With John being meticulous he had kept Roger Tissler's number. He thought what the hell, so he rang him.

"Hello, Roger?" he said. "Roger?"

"John Gammon. Blimey that's a coincidence I was only talking to the wife about you. We are in the Peak District for a few days, we have a caravan at Pommie Grange. Had it for a few years John. How are you keeping? I heard you had settled in the Peak District. Weren't you from round there?"

"Yes mate, from near Hittington."

"Well what a co-incidence, me and the wife walked from Hittington past that Roman settlement and ended up in Ropesmoor. Absolutely stunning scenery. So are you still in the Police force? Mind you are a lot younger than me. I retired two years back. I was fifty nine, so I thought what the hell. We bought this caravan and it's a lovely site and I get my wi-fi so I'm happy."

"Yes mate, still working as a DI in Bixton. I rang because I wondered if you could help me?"

"If I can lad, you know that."

"Could we meet tomorrow?"

"Yes, what time?"

"Say 12.00 noon. I'll treat you and
your good lady to lunch at the Derby
Ram. It's right on that bad bend
going through Pommie."

"Oh, it's lovely there, John. A bit
expensive though, are you sure?"

"Definitely Roger, see you there
mate."

"Ok John, lovely to hear from
you."

The phone went dead so John
made some notes. If anybody could
get into Brian Lund's bank accounts
and e-mails etc it was old Anorak he
thought.

The following day John headed for
the picturesque village of Pommie. It
had a massive church which stood
majestically on the first part of the
High Street. The paths were all

THE CURE

cobbled and the main High Street twisted and turned its way through the village like an enormous python.

As John drove into the village he thought to himself how lucky this village was; with small bakers, two butchers, a grocery store and post office combined and three pubs.

All the houses that hung on the roadside had been either lead miners' cottages or quarryman's' cottages. Although those industries had gone, the men of the village now had work in the surrounding towns at the new industrial estates that had shot up everywhere.

John parked his car in the Derby Ram. He had to drive through an archway to access the car park then walk back to the front of the building. Its claim to fame was that Queen Victoria had to stay there one winter's night when the snow had got so bad. John Lennon and George Harrison had reputedly stayed there in the sixties when the Beatles were playing at Bixton Palace Hotel.

John entered the first room which wasn't particularly big but seemed very welcoming with its little coal fire fully stacked with logs and coal. He could see through to the back room and he could see Roger Tissler and his wife by the bigger log fire. Roger hadn't aged much John thought, although he was white now instead of the jet-black hair he remembered.

"Roger?"

"Hello John, so nice to see you. This is my wife, Angela."

Angela put out her hand to John.

"Nice to meet you John."

"Have you got a drink?"

"No, not yet. We were a little early and the landlord asked if we could give him a minute as he was doing the fire in the other end.

"Ok, what would you like?"

"I'll have a half of Pommie bitter please, John."

"And for you Angela?"

"Just a slim line tonic, no ice but with a slice please, John."

John could not resist a pint of Lead Miners. He used to drink that years ago with Steve in the Tow'd Man when they were only sixteen. It seemed fitting to have one for his mate.

John returned with the drinks.

"Cheers John, and it's a real pleasure to be in your company."

"Not sure you will think that when I ask you for my favour."

"Fire away lad, what is it?"

"Well I need to look at somebody's emails and bank accounts."

"Oh, I'm not sure about that John. I don't dabble anymore, not that I ever did it for gain anyway."

"I know that Roger, but I need to tell you the reason over lunch."

A young girl arrived to take the order.

"I'm going to have a Derbyshire oatcake with cheese, spring onion and chopped black pudding on a bed of rocket salad with baby new potatoes. Ok, Angela, Roger?"

"I think I will try Pommie Feta Tart with baby new potatoes and Pommie allotment vegetables."

"I think I will have the same Roger, sounds grand does that."

The girl went off with the order and John told the story of his mate and the fire. and the death of Jo and Leah Marie. It made Angela shed a tear.

THE CURE

"Oh, how awful for the poor man, and now he is being framed for their murders. You have to help John. Roger, this isn't fair."

"Well John, if the lady that wears the trousers says I have to do something, I know better than to argue."

"Ok Roger, do you want to come to mine tomorrow and work on it for me?"

"Ok lad, write down your address. We have sat nav in the car. Shall we say 9.30am, John?"

"That's good for me mate."

The food arrived and within no time it was devoured by all three.

"Tell you what John, we will come here again, that was lovely."

"Good Angela, pleased you enjoyed it."

"Let us pay our way, John."

"Wouldn't dream of it. I really appreciate your help for my friend."

John left the Tisslers contemplating another drink. It was now almost 3.00pm so John decided to pop and see Saron.

The Tow'd Man was quite busy. They had a walking party in from Derby, Donna told him. He ordered a pint then asked after Saron.

"She has just gone to see her mum, John. She said she will be back about 5.00pm. She isn't cooking tonight so she said if I needed a hand behind the bar she would be here, but if not she was having a drink your side. She is a workaholic John. She hasn't had a proper day off in ages, so I have no intention of asking for help tonight."

John was sitting at the bar when Phil Sterndale and Sheba Filey came in. They had been to some farmers market looking at beast as Phil called them.

"What are you two having?"

"I'll have a Winksworth Blonde please, John."

"Can I have double vodka and skinny coke please, John?"

"Not a problem coming straight up."

John ordered the drinks and they sat chatting. A few drinks later and Saron appeared looking gorgeous as ever in a blue dress, a cream cropped cardigan and cream shoes, with just a single string of pearls round her neck to compliment the dress.

"Come and join us, Saron."

"I think I will, Sheba."

Saron sat next to John and Donna brought her a double brandy and coke.

"Blimey, this feels nice relaxing not worrying about the pub, Sheba."

"I bet. We have just been to Gawburton to a farmers market. Phil is stocking up his farm, so I said I would tag along. You can't beat breakfast at these farmers markets."

By 9.00pm they were all well on their way. Phil said that he and Sheba were calling it a night. He had some guys coming to erect a shed at 8.30am in the morning, and said he needed his wits about him.

Other than the four of them the pub was quiet. Saron told Donna she could go to her flat, and she would lock up at 10.00pm if nobody else came in.

At spot on ten she locked the doors. Her speech was slightly slurred when she asked John to stay. This absolutely made his day. He checked the fires and the windows

THE CURE

and Saron said she would see him upstairs.

He eventually climbed the stairs. Saron had taken a bottle of Moet in an ice bucket, and was laying on the bed in a white flimsy lace top with white stockings and suspenders and a pair of white high heels. John's eyes almost popped out of his head.

He lay on the bed next to her caressing the nape of her neck. Slowly as she writhed in pleasure. He turned her over and slowly worked his way down her back. Saron seemed ecstatic. She moved round to see John.

"I do love you," she said.

"Well you know I love you, don't you?"

"Why are you so stupid then John. Am I not enough for you?"

"Of course you are. All I think about is you."

"Then why the other girls?"

"I don't know. Insecurity, I know I can't use Lindsay as an excuse forever, but she did mess my head up, Saron."

They made love and lust in equal measures before lying back on the bed. John kissed Saron passionately.

"Can we try again, Saron?"

"I don't know John. I am not sure I am ready. It upset Mum so much that she hasn't been the same since the wedding day, John."

"I am so sorry for what I did the night before, but the car accident I can't be blamed for," he said passing her a glass of Moet.

They carried on talking until the early hours when Saron fell asleep on John.

THE CURE

It was 9.15am when John glanced over at the bedside clock. Saron was still asleep on him.

"Crap! Sorry Saron, I have an important meeting at 9.30am. I have to go."

He kissed her and hurriedly put on his shirt and trousers and left thinking he would have a shower after his meeting with Roger.

He arrived at Hittington just as Roger was pulling out of the drive.

"Look, I am so sorry mate."

"No problem mate, I thought I must have put the address wrong in the sat nav."

John showed Roger into the cottage. Thank goodness Phyllis had been cleaning the day before so it looked ok.

"Nice place you have, John."

"Well these were sheds because this was all Mum and Dad's farm.

When they died I was left these so did them up and I rent the rest as holiday lets and live in this one."

"That's worth knowing. I wouldn't mind a week down here, it's absolutely stunning scenery."

"Not a problem mate. Give me a call when you have spoken with Angela and I will makes sure one is free for you, on the house."

"Hey, no John we would have to pay."

"Trust me, if what I think you can do to help Steve then that is payment enough, mate."

"Ok let's get stated. I hope you don't mind, I have brought my own lap top. I can drive it better. I just need the code for your internet."

John scrabbled about in the kitchen draw to find his network key code and gave it to Roger who by now had his laptop open waiting.

THE CURE

"Right John, what would you like me to hack into?"

"Ok, a Mr Brian Lund."

Roger set about the task. He was incredible to watch as he darted between programs.

"John, I have three Brian Lunds; one in Dorset, one in Derby and one in Stoke on Trent."

"Go with the Derby one first."

Lund had accounts with HSBC and Santander.

"Ok, the HSBC is protected so it might take about twenty minutes to unlock it, John."

"No problem, Roger would you like a coffee and a piece of Phyllis Swan's homemade coffee and ginger cake?"

"Sounds great John, just one sugar in my coffee, please mate."

By the time John got back with the cake and drinks Roger had cracked it.

"Right young Mr Lund, let's see what was so private. John, he has a regular amount paid into his account by the Home Office. How bizarre, is this man working for the government?"

"Not how you think mate. Between me and you he is a nasty piece of work, but I have been told on numerous occasions that I have to drop any cases against him. If what I think, he is involved in Jo's and her little girl's murder, then I am having him one way or another, mate."

"Well he receives three thousand and eighty pounds on the first of every month, John."

Gammon made notes.

"Anything else, Roger?"

THE CURE

"Nothing untoward on this account. He has a big mortgage payment of almost three grand which I am guessing is why the Home Office payments are sent to this account. Bit sloppy on his part, John."

"Agree, but if his accounts were protected normally we would have to apply to the courts to see them. He knows they would knock it back, so he thinks he is safe."

"Right, let's look at the Santander account. Straight in here mate. It looks like he makes regular payments into a high interest account. That's if there is such a thing these days," and Roger laughed.

"Looks like this is purely a savings account."

"Does the money go in same day every time?"

"No John, it's random over the month."

"What have the last three months payments in been?"

"Just a second. December, seventeen thousand and fifty five pounds. January, sixty one thousand pounds and so far this month eight thousand and thirty three pounds."

"How much is totally in the account?"

"Wow, you would not believe this John. One and a half million quid."

"Anything else?"

"No, nothing John."

"Ok mate, have a go at the Brian Lund in Stoke on Trent. I think it's one and the same."

"Ok John, he has one account with The Potteries Building Society and one with Nat West. I'll start off with the Building Society. Straight in mate. He has thirty three thousand pounds in this account, but no transactions in or out, other than this money in October 2015. Bit weird, it's like he has forgot he has it, John."

"Right Roger, interesting. Let's look at Nat West."

"Same again mate, locked, just give me a bit of time."

"Not a problem."

Four hours passed before Roger finally got in the account.

"Bingo, we are in mate."

"Bloody hell, I can see why this was so secure."

"Why Roger?"

"There are payments here from famous people."

"Who like?"

"Sir Michael Sudbury, Home Secretary I believe, Julian Mansell Defence Secretary, if I'm not mistaken. TV host Robert Thurlow, he is the guy that does that political program on BBC on a Sunday evening. Oh, and look at this one, HRH Henry Prince of Wales."

"Bloody hell, what are these payments for? How much are they?"

"Well there are a lot, and most are in the twelve hundred pounds region, John."

"Any wonder he is protected, Roger. Don't breathe a word of this Roger, its dangerous information."

"Once I put my lap top down, I have finished John. I won't breathe a word."

"Let's take a quick look at Brian Lund in Dorset."

"Just one account John, with RBS. This is a different bloke, his name is Brian Alexander Lund, and it's just a general account, you know, every day bills etc nothing major."

THE CURE

"Ok Roger, well thank you so much for all this information. I have written it down and when I use it, don't worry, your name will not be involved. Don't forget you ever want a holiday let then give me a call. Here's my number and you and your wife can stay for as long as you want on me. Roger, I really appreciate your help."

"Anytime mate, it's been great to see you, it really has."

Roger left, so John sat and did a small report on all the information. His next task was how he could implicate the brothers and hopefully Lund in the deaths of Jo and Lea Marie.

He just made himself another coffee when his mobile rang. It was DCI Dirk.

"John?"

"Hello Sir."

JOHN GAMMON PEAK DISTRICT DETECTIVE
Series Three Book Two

"I have just rung Stoke for you, but they tell me you have phoned in sick?"

"Yes, a been a bit of colour Sir."

"Call me cynical if you wish, but I hope your sickness isn't related to the Lineman case?"

John didn't answer.

"Are you fit for work tomorrow?"

"Yes, should be Sir."

"Good, I need you back at Bixton. We have had another case of a young girl murdered."

"Blimey, that's a quick change of heart."

"Maybe I like you where I can see you, Gammon. See you in the morning," and Dirk hung up.

Damn John thought, but at least I have some information. I will just have to work on it during the weekends.

THE CURE

John knew about the dead girl as DI Smarty had told him the night before.

The following morning John headed back to Bixton, secretly pleased at what Roger had got for him. He wished Fleur would ring him, she would know more about what was going on.

"Good morning Sir, good to see you back."

"Thank you, Sergeant Beeney."

"We certainly need some help, what with another girl found dead, and now that elderly couple at Pommie found dead in their caravan."

"Sorry, what did you say?"

"Sorry sir, I thought you knew. All the detectives are at Pommie. There has been a fire and a couple's caravan was burned while they were inside late last night. The fire brigade were called and they contacted us. Both the male and the female had their throats cut.

John was dreading what he was thinking. Was it Roger and Angela Tissler?

"Ok, I'm going up there, Sergeant."

John raced to the caravan park at Pommie. As he parked he could see John Walvin's forensic tent and the DI's milling about. As John got closer he could see it was Roger and Angela's caravan. He felt so upset that he had created this situation for such a lovely couple. This is Lund he thought. He must monitor his accounts somehow, and he will have been able to trace who entered the site. Guessing he is an ex copper he probably thought he was doing private investigation work. John felt sick to the pit of his stomach. This can't go on he thought, he had to address the Lund situation.

Gammon knew now he was on a real sticky wicket with his superiors. If he reported what Roger had found, then he would be in a real pile of brown stuff as a serving police officer. His evidence would be admissible in a court of law as it was obtained illegally.

John had seen enough. He was intent on revenge and decided to drive to the Drovers Arms in Derby to see if Lund was in.

He parked his car on some waste land near the pub and strode with purpose over to the pub. There were a few drinkers in. Luckily for John, in a corner with two women draped over him, was Lund with two heavies.

"Hey, look lads," Lund shouted, "Its old Johnny Boy come to see his master."

Gammon couldn't help himself and ran to grab Lund. He felt a sudden smack across his back and then one to his head. Gammon came round in a back room tied to a chair.

Lund sat across from Gammon laughing.

"You are in serious trouble now, Lund."

"Listen to the puppy bark, lads. What do you reckon?"

Gammon struggled but couldn't free himself from his shackles.

"What did you come to see your old mate for, Johnny Boy?"

"You are not my mate, Lund. I know you killed my friend and his wife."

"Really don't know what you are banging on about, Gammon."

THE CURE

Gammon knew he had hit a raw bone by the way Lund spoke.

"Let me tell you what is going to happen here, shall I? Young Piers here will inject you with a massive amount of heroin. You will then be taken to somewhere in the Peak District and dumped. You will have a prostitute's knickers in your pocket and a couple of girl's calling cards. Oh, and by the way, they will say you use them all the time and they also get you drugs. So, you see Johnny Boy, you are stuffed. Nobody will believe you about anything. You silly little prat. You will need a job after this, and I am looking for a gardener," and Lund laughed.

He turned to the first guy.

"Leroy, go with Piers and make sure you carry out my instructions to the letter."

Lund left and Gammon tried to dissuade the brothers from carrying out his orders.

"You do know you will be in prison for life for this, don't you?"

Piers laughed as he flicked the needle containing the heroin. Leroy held Gammon's hand while Piers pushed the needle into Gammon's vein. Gammon almost immediately went into a stupor.

"Ok, push these stained knickers in his pocket and these two business cards."

Gammon could hear them, but it was like he was floating above looking down. In the van he could hear Leroy saying that Piers should not have started the fire that Lund wasn't too happy to lose a key supplier. John took it to mean Jo was dealing for Lund. Now he knew Steve hadn't done what he was being charged with. John had more pressing things to think about. After about half an hour Leroy and Piers pulled onto some bumpy land, and Gammon heard the brothers say here will do. Gammon could see a tyre jack laying on the floor. With every sinew of strength he had, he waited for the brothers to drag him out, and hit them both across the temple. Leroy fell back instantly, but he had not quite hit Piers as good, although enough to daze him. He could feel himself coming in and out of consciousness, but again he hit Piers full on in the face. This time he went down. John struggled to his feet. He didn't know if the men were dead or not, and he didn't particularly care. He staggered across what appeared to be moorland. He could see a bright light in the distance so decided to head for that.

John hadn't got a clue how he
would get out of this, but he needed
help and quick.

In life, sometimes somebody is
looking down on you at your
blackest hour. The light he had seen
was the Tow'd Man. John banged on
the door. A window upstairs opened.

"John, oh no John, wait I'm
coming down."

It was Saron. She rushed
downstairs and helped John in. She
tried to talk with him, but the drug
had taken its affect, so she helped
upstairs to a bed. John managed to
say heroin in a garbled tone.

Saron called John Walvin and told
him to come to the pub. She needed
help and quick. She told Wally that
she thought John had overdosed on
heroin but to say nothing to anyone.

THE CURE

Wally arrived and quickly got to work on John. He stayed through the night while John went through hell.

The following morning John was being sick when Saron noticed the knickers sticking out of his coat. She made him take his coat off and looked in his pockets where she found the two prostitutes cards.

She showed them to Wally.

"Look Saron, just wait. Let's get John back in the real world then he might be able to tell us what happened."

"Well this is one story I can't wait to hear from John Gammon's mouth, Wally."

Wally had phoned work to say he was ill. Saron said John had relapsed, and he was still ill so would not be in.

They sat drinking coffee. Donna said she would sort the pub, and she had put a 'no food today' due to kitchen problems.

John said his head was killing him. He explained what had happened and what he could remember.

By 4.00pm he was feeling a bit better. Donna came up to say two men had been found dead on the moor.

"Now the fun begins," said Wally.

"Look John, don't panic. I will go onto the moor say I was on my way to work feeling better. Then I can check the bodies for DNA or any clues you had even been there."

"Look Wally, I am so sorry to put you in this position."

"John if they killed Jo and her daughter they deserved what they got. We aren't losing the Peak District's best ever detective through these scumbags."

THE CURE

Wally left and John was feeling quite lousy. Saron made him some chicken broth, and then John explained all that had happened.

"Surely they can't let this Lund character get away with what they have, John?"

"He was instrumental in my brother's death, my mother's death and quite sure everything with Adam brought on my father's heart attack and his untimely death. Not forgetting all those people killed in the safe house. He has connections very high up. My friend from when I was serving in London came to my house and helped me break into Lund's accounts, and it's shocking the amount of money that man has. Between me and you Saron, he is also getting paid by some very high-ranking ministers etc hence the protection I believe."

John wanted to tell Saron
everything, and also about his step
sister, but he thought he better not.

It was now 8.00pm and John was
feeling a bit better, although he felt
as if he was starting with man-flu.
John knew he had to make work
tomorrow. With the death of the two
men who he killed, he had to be sure
nothing led to him.

Saron came up at 11.45pm and
John was fast asleep, so she went in
the other room. John had set his
alarm for 6.30am in case he was still
feeling dreadful, and it took longer to
come round. He needed to burn the
clothes he had worn that night, and
shower and put new clothes on for
work.

His alarm sounded and he didn't
feel too bad, so he left Saron a

THE CURE

message saying thank you for everything and he left for his cottage.

John put his clothes and shoes in a bin liner and quickly burned them in the small leaf burner he had bought for the garden. Then he showered, changed, then headed for Bixton and work.

DCI Dirk had called a meeting in the incident room and as Gammon walked in he sarcastically said, "Here is our prodigal son."

DI Smarty deflected the comment by clapping. Scooper and the rest also clapped and said how pleased they were to have him back on the team. This pretty much put DCI Dirk in his place.

"Right, listen up everyone, it's been mental. We have a couple found at the caravan place called Pommie Grange. They had their throats slit and the caravan set on fire. Mr Walvin fill us in please.

"Well, we have looked into it and through dental records we found that their names were Roger and Angela Tissler. Roger was a former police officer in London."

"Yes, Scooper?"

"I contacted the owners of Pommie Grange, and they said they came regularly to the site. They both enjoyed walking and were an all-round nice couple."

Dirk put their pictures up and pictures of the burnt-out caravan. John felt incensed at the injustice.

"Now, two males found bludgeoned on Elton Moor last night with a white butcher's van with writing on the side. What did you find Mr Walvin?"

Wally stood up. This was the bit John was dreading.

THE CURE

"The two men, again by dental records and DNA, were Leroy Gabble and a Piers Gabble, both in their mid-thirties both with criminal records. They had both been hit with a heavy object. Leroy Gabble had been hit just the once at the side of the temple and Piers Gabble had been hit once with what appeared to be a glancing blow and then once full on in the face. This didn't kill him but he had fell back onto a lump of concrete, and that is what killed him."

"I found traces of DNA which were from Jo Wickets. We also found cans in the butcher's van that had some fuel in, but just residue. They had been used, I believe, in the murder of Jo wickets and her daughter.

DCI Dirk, who now was feeling a bit embarrassed, asked Wally if his findings would stand up to in-depth investigation?

Wally said yes.

"So, we now have the problem of why was Jo Wickets and her daughter murdered and why were these two scumbags murdered? It looks like the scumbags did the deed at the Wicket house. I assume they were killed when a drug bust went wrong. Gammon's heart was racing. I will inform CPS, but I doubt they will use police resources to find out who killed the scumbags. I will also get Mr Lineman released and explain the full extent of what happened."

"So, with that out of the way, what about the Mandy bellow murder?"

Wally stood up again.

"There is no doubt our bleach killer has struck again, Sir. We found traces of bleach to the same levels of the other three victims. It's like he is metering the exact quantity every time he kills."

"Ok John," and he turned to Gammon.

"I want you to shake some trees on the suspects we have in this bleach case. I better go and get an innocent man freed."

John could have hugged Wally. It was him and only him that had saved the day.

After the meeting Gammon hung back to thank Wally.

"I can't thank you enough, Wally. I made a schoolboy mistake going after Lund, and it almost cost me my career and my liberty."

"John, no thanks needed, just doing my job," and he smiled like only Wally could and left the room.

John sat thinking in the quiet for a minute. He knew he had been lucky,

in fact very lucky, He also knew that
Lund was a formidable opponent and
he had to find another way to bring
him down, and the corrupt
establishment that backed him.

Gammon went back to his office
to decide on a plan to get this bleach
maniac. John sat at his desk
scribbling on his pad the names of
the victims on one side, then the
suspects on the other side. Gammon
had done this many times over the
years. It often made his mind think
out of the box.

Right he thought. Time to get
moving He called down to Sergeant
Beeney to get everyone in the
incident room at 4.00pm.

Gammon stood looking across at
Losehill when his phone rang,

"John?"

"Steve, they will let you out."

THE CURE

"I know, just been told mate. I am guessing it's down to you."

"What time will you be let out, Steve?

"That's why I rang mate. Can you pick me up outside the prison at 9.00am?"

"Of course I will mate."

Now John had too think how much he told Steve. Did he tell him who killed Jo and his daughter? Did he tell him the house and things were all down to possibly drug money?

Scooper put her head round his office door.

"Are you coming to the meeting you called, John?"

"Oh yeah, sorry Sandra."

John followed her down to the incident room where everyone was assembled.

"Ok, tomorrow DI Smarty take DS Yap and let's bring in Mark Block for questioning., DI Scooper you and Sergeant Magic bring in Andrew Firm. DI Lee you over-see this and arrange court orders to check out their properties."

"DI Smarty can you hold back? I need a word. Can you cover me? I should be in about 11.00am. I am picking Steve up."

"No problem John, pleased he is out mate. Bad enough losing his family without being blamed for the murders."

It was the end of the shift so Gammon left Bixton. He needed to get some new tea towels. Phyllis Swan had said the ones he had were beyond redemption.

John called into a Wilko's on the way home and picked some up. It

THE CURE

was a job Phyllis would normally do for him, but she was going to Bruges for four days. He did a small shop as well for deodorant, shaving foam and cleaning products.

On the way back he rang Saron to thank her again for helping him. He was a bit surprised at her reaction. He thought he was making headways with her, but she seemed distant again, and didn't want to speak. With this in mind he headed for the Spinning Jenny.

It was 6.30pm when he arrived. Kev was sitting at the end of the bar with a bottle of low calorie lager. Anouska was behind the bar and there were a few people waiting to go through to the restaurant.

"Pedigree for John please, Anouska."

"Very kind of you Kev."

"We have to look after the locals
you know," and he laughed.

"Rum do all these murders, John."

John smiled knowing that now he
not only arrested bad guys, but had
actually killed some bad guys.

"I hear those two drug dealers
were close to the Tow'd Man. I hope
Saron and Donna were ok?"

"Yes, they were Kev. I have been
seeing a bit of Saron, so was at the
Tow'd Man that night."

"Anyway, enough of that Kev. I
am picking Steve up from Leicester
prison in the morning."

"John that's great news. So, you
proved it wasn't Steve?"

"Yes mate, and a lot more that I
can't divulge."

"Well done lad. Look John, best
finish this. I promised Doreen I
would take her to Bixton Opera
House tonight to see that comedian

THE CURE

Mickey Slowhand. We are going with Bob and Cheryl. I think Bob is after some new material."

"Ok Kev, have a good night."

"Will do mate."

It was 9.30pm and John decided to have one last drink. Anouska poured him a double brandy. The pub was empty except John and Anouska. Kev had told her to lock up at ten if nobody was in.

As it was now ten Anouska announced she was locking up.

"You can't. I'm here and I am a paying customer, Anouska."

She smiled and brought a bottle of brandy round from the bar.

"Then I suggest, naughty Mr Gammon, that we drink this together. What would you like on the music machine?"

John was a bit taken back and just said anything.

After a further two double brandies. Anouska had told him of her life back home and was coming on quite strong. She started to tease him, rubbing her perfectly formed hands up and down his leg. This was one sexy girl John thought. Anouska stood up John could see her body through the sheer top she was wearing. Anouska pulled John towards her by his tie and started kissing and caressing him all over.

"Let's go to your room, Anouska. I don't want Kev and Doreen catching us at it down here."

"It's more dangerous, Mr Gammon," she said in a sultry voice and laughed.

They entered her room and she pounced on John leaving him under no illusion about what was about to happen. She straddled John telling him not to do anything until she said.

THE CURE

Halfway through he started thinking about Saron, but this girl was most men's dreams he thought. Almost one hour passed. When it was over, and whilst the night was good with Anouska, John's thoughts were with Saron. Anouska fell asleep and John lay wide awake thinking of Saron. He heard Kev and Doreen come in. Kev sounded drunk as Doreen was pushing him along the corridor.

CHAPTER FIVE

John woke at 5.00am and left Anouska fast asleep and drove home. He didn't want to bump into Doreen.

John showered and changed, and set off to pick Steve up from Leicester Prison. It was with some trepidation. He just hoped Steve understood why he couldn't visit.

John arrived, and Steve was standing outside the big gates. He had lost a lot of weight and was sporting a black eye.

"Get in, Steve."

"Thanks, John."

"What happened with the eye, mate?"

"Oh, fell over."

"Yeah, likely story."

"You should see the guy who I fell over," and Steve laughed.

THE CURE

"Good to see you have not lost your sense of humour, mate."

"I'm starving John, any chance we can pull over to get a breakfast? That prison food was atrocious."

John pulled in to a small café called the Laughing Hen. It looked ok from the outside. They sat at a window table and pleasant guy in his mid-sixties came over. When the guy smiled he had the biggest gap in his front teeth.

"Right, what can I get you?" he said looking at John, then turning to Steve.

"Bet you want a piece of steak for that eye, lad?"

"No, just a mega breakfast for me, old lad," Steve said.

"And for you?"

"Same for me mate," John replied.

"So, tell me John how did you manage to get me out of prison?"

Now John had to decide how he told Steve about Jo and who was involved in her killing. Because, as sure as eggs are eggs, he would go after Lund.

"Look mate, as painful as this might seem, I need to tell you something."

"Fire away mate, you know me."

"That's the problem Steve, I do know you and you have to let me do this my way."

"Ok, ok just tell me."

"I contacted a mate from my days down in London, and a stroke of luck, he was staying at The Grange in Pommie. He had a caravan there. Anyway, this guy was an absolute wizard on computers and can hack into anything. Without going into too much detail, he found a load of stuff on a guy in Derby, who we have monitored for many years. It sadly cost him and his wife their lives."

"What for me, John?"

"Sadly mate, yes."

"Because I was so mad about it, I went to see the guy in Derby. I wasn't thinking straight, and this guy is a dangerous man. I bust into where he drinks, and before I know it his two heavies have me tied up. They injected me with an overdose of heroin, stuffed a pair of soiled prostitutes knickers in my pockets, along with a couple of the prostitutes' business cards."

"Why do that mate?"

"I believe they were going to dump me to die, and then any evidence would have been discounted as my reputation would have been gone."

They drove me out, and I was out of it Steve. I was drifting in and out

of consciousness. When the van
pulled up I knew it was now or
never. I hit the first guy with a tyre
jack but the other guy I had to hit
twice. You must never repeat this
Steve. I killed them both."

Steve sat listening intensely.

"These two men killed Jo and
Leah Marie."

Steve broke down just as the old
guy arrived with the biggest
breakfast you could imagine. Four
sausages, two black pudding slices,
four rashers of bacon, three eggs,
four hash browns, a large portion of
fried mash potato, two slices of fried
bread, mushrooms, tomatoes, beans
and four slices of crusty bread cut
like doorsteps.

"Blimey lad"

"Don't get upset if it's not big
enough, I'll do you some more."

Steve recomposed himself.

THE CURE

"No, it's ok. It's his bloody jokes, they make me cry."

The guy dropped the breakfast and two pint mugs of tea.

"John, I owe you so much, but I do need to know who was behind Jo's death and why?"

John thought for a minute but held back telling him the truth about Jo.

"In good time mate, now get your breakfast, I have to get back to work mate."

"Well thanks again John, you have always been a good mate."

He arrived at Bixton feeling he had done something wrong with Anouska. He should not have felt like this, Saron hadn't really forgiven him, but he just did.

John dropped Steve off at Tracey Rodgers Lodge and headed for Bixton. He walked into the station.

Desk Sergeant Beeney said it had been a rough night in Bixton.

"What was the problem?"

"Oh, fighting. Bixton played Micklock and it all kicked off, Sir."

Gammon really wasn't interested, that was something the beat lads could sort. Gammon made his way upstairs to his office. He had just sat down at his desk when he got a text. It was Beth. It just said, 'thank you John, yes let him know please'.

Knowing how important this would be to Carl, he rang him.

"Carl, can you come to my office?"

A few minutes passed and Carl knocked on Gammon's door.

"Come in."

DI Milton entered Gammon's office.

"What's the problem, John?"

"Sit down, Carl."

THE CURE

"First of all, I need you to be aware that what I am about to tell you must forever be between us, this must never be compromised."

"You have found Beth, haven't you John?"

"I have, Carl."

Carl looked at John for which seemed like an eternity before sobbing. Poor Carl was so upset he just starting sobbing.

"Have you spoken to her, John?"

"Yes, mate."

"So, what did she say?"

"She misses you mate. She deliberately let you see her, but at the last minute bottled it."

"What do you mean, John?"

"Try and understand, Carl. She survived everything, but the price she had to pay was to lose you and her good friend Joni. She had to go to another safe house, just in case those evil men worked out what had happened."

"John, she had a funeral and left me thinking she was dead. Do you know how I have felt?"

"Look Carl, what you do with this is down to you. I have purely tried to help you."

"I'm sorry John, thank you so much, and I will never repeat what you have told me."

Gammon wrote down the address and pushed it across the desk. Carl folded the piece of paper and put it in his inside pocket. He stood up and thanked John and left. Gammon wasn't sure if telling him was the right thing to do but it was done now.

By 1.00pm Gammon had his post done and was just considering nipping into Bixton for a sandwich when his mobile rang.

THE CURE

"Mr Loser, good afternoon."

Gammon knew straight away who it was. The serial killer was taunting.

"I'm unsure why I am your contact, but you can rest assured that I will get you."

"You are all wrong about me. So, you really think I am a common serial killer? No Loser, it's all about research. I will find the cure, but I have to let you and the stupid media think I am some kind of psychopath. That means you and the rest of your police force leave people like me alone, Loser."

"Look, I don't know what you mean by cure, but let me help you. Come into the police station and give yourself up, instead of murdering all these people. It sounds like you are convinced that you are trying to find a cure for something or somebody, but it's misguided."

As Gammon said misguided the caller rang off.

Gammon immediately went to see DCI Dirk and filled him in about the telephone call from killer. Dirk seemed distant.

"John, can I just apologise for getting your friend banged up? I have to say it's resting heavy on me. The two guys who did this, something doesn't quite add up. I have been racking my brain over it."

"Sir, with the greatest respect, those scum bags were drug dealers, and some other scum bags killed them. I am guessing a drug bust went wrong. They killed my friend and his daughter. I am sorry, but I feel nothing for them, we need to concentrate on this serial killer."

"You are correct John, we just don't seem to be getting anywhere. Have you any new ideas?"

THE CURE

"Cases like this seem to be always on the side of the perpetrator, then they make a mistake."

"I know and if anybody can crack a serial killer case it's you, John."

Meanwhile Carl Milton had told Sergeant Beeney he had a dental appointment, but he was going to find Beth. Carl's heart was racing as he drove into the quaint village of Pommie. Carl parked a little away from the address John had given him. He didn't want Beth to see him until she opened the front door in case she changed her mind and ran again. Then he would never see her ever again he thought.

Carl's heart was beating so fast he felt like it was about to jump out of his chest. Carl knocked on the small cottage door. His expectations were

running so high he felt like he was
about to faint. A few seconds past
but it felt like minutes. Eventually
Beth came to the door. They just
stood looking at each other for a few
moments before Beth fell into Carl's
arms sobbing.

"I have missed you so much, Carl.
I am so sorry, I thought I could do
this, but I am so lonely and have
missed you so much. Come inside
quickly. Let me make a drink. Still
coffee, white, two sugars?"

"Yes please, Beth."

They talked and talked for almost
four hours. Beth told Carl she
wanted a normal life, but she was
scared of involving him again. This
might mean they come after her and
him. Eventually Beth said he was to
leave.

"Call me Beth, please."

THE CURE

"I will, but I need to think this through."

Carl kissed her passionately and left. Beth shut her door almost immediately. Carl wasn't sure if it had gone well, but he had to hope. He noticed he had twelve missed calls from John Gammon. Carl sat in his car and phoned Gammon.

"I am guessing you didn't have a dental appointment, but you have gone to see Beth."

"Sorry, John."

"How did it go?"

"She is going to call me."

"Well you can't expect much more at this point, can you?"

"I just want to be with her, John."

"Carl, I can't see how you can be with her and live round here. Too many people know her. If they are still looking for her, and it appears they must be because they moved her so quickly, then I would suggest that if you want to be with her, you get as far away from the Peak District as possible. See me when you get back, Carl," and the call ended.

Carl arrived back at the station and went straight to John's office.

"Come in Carl, I think we should have this chat. DCI Dirk is on holiday for a week and a bloody good job."

"I can't help my feelings and I'm not going to lose her even for my career. I took on board your thoughts John, and you are not wrong. We have to get away, and to that end I am going back now to sort with Beth."

"I am only giving you the advice I did as a friend, Carl."

"I know John. Look, I am going back now," and Carl left.

THE CURE

Gammon was beginning to have regrets that he had told Carl. It was clear he was determined to be with Beth and that meant Bixton losing a first-class detective. Not wise on his part he thought.

Gammon started on his paperwork when Sergeant Beeney rang.

"Sir, we have just taken a call from a Derbyshire medic. They were called out today to a suspected suicide. Some guy who lives nearby was delivering logs to the man's house. He said he lifted the garage door and found him swinging from a beam."

"Do we have a name of the victim?"

"The guy delivering logs said it was David Sowers."

"Ok Sergeant, get DI Smarty tell him to meet me at my car."

Gammon put his coat on and raced down the stairs to his car. After the conversation with the killer maybe it was Sowers, and he had a guilty conscience and decided to take his own life.

On the way out he had instructed Beeney to get John Walvin and the team over there fast.

Gammon and Smarty set off.

"What's the crack with young, Carl John? He seems totally off kilter at the minute."

"It's a long story, Dave."

Just has Gammon said the words the phone rang, and it was Carl. He sounded dreadful.

"She isn't here, John. She has gone, I know it they have moved her again."

"Look Carl, get over to Winksworth, we have a situation and I will be able to talk to you. The address is The Lead Miner's Cottage, The Dale. Oh, and Carl stop in the car. I can hear you are upset and it's best if we chat in your car."

"Ok John, thank you."

Smarty and Gammon arrived at the cottage and were met by Phil Sterndale.

"Phil, what are you doing here?"

"I do a bit of logging and sell them on the side. This guy rang up and wanted a tonne dropping. He said if he wasn't in, the garage would be open. I backed the truck up and knocked at the door, but nobody answered. I thought I haven't got time to muck about, so I raised the garage door. That's when I found him. He was hanging from a beam and a chair was on its side John, so he had just kicked the chair away it looks like."

"Did you cut him down, or the paramedics, Phil?"

"I cut him down. I thought I might be able to save him because he wasn't blue. I wondered if it was a cry for help with him saying drop the logs in the garage."

"Did you know him, Phil?"

"No, not really. He had logs last winter, but I don't get up to Winksworth much. I don't really know anybody much up there, John."

"Ok Phil, are you ok?"

"Yes mate, things like this don't bother me too much to be honest."

"Ok, well I may need to ask you to pop in depending on what we find here Phil, but you are ok to get on delivering those logs."

"You don't fancy giving me a hand with deliveries then mate?" and Sterndale laughed.

THE CURE

"Think I will take a rain-check on that."

While Gammon had been talking Wally and the crew had arrived to set up.

"What do you reckon, John?"

"I took a call yesterday Dave from the killer, and he was basically saying he wasn't a murderer. It was more like clinical trials."

"Bloody nut case."

"Think I agree Dave. I tried to talk him into giving himself up, but he rang off. I just wonder if it was this guy, and he decided to end it all. When he was sentenced to thirty years all that time ago for using bleach on those teenagers, he said at his trial that in years to come he would be proved right. That bleach would be used as a bodily cleaning agent."

"Ok, let's take a look in his house to see if we can find any clues to this mess."

Gammon pushed in the rear door. The house was a bit of a mess with a sink full of pots, breadcrumbs from the toaster on the side and the floor was sticky. The living room had no family pictures, but there was one of Sowers standing next to an old Ford Cortina MK2 in flared trousers and a penny collar shirt with a Fair Isle pullover, and he was smiling. That picture was on his mantlepiece.

"Bloody hell John, I dressed like that in the seventies, and my brother had a Mk 2 Cortina in the same colour as that."

"Ok, cut the nostalgia, let's get some evidence that this was our man."

Gammon headed upstairs while Smarty went in the cellar. The first room appeared to be Sowers bedroom. The bed was made but it had an old-fashioned candlewick bed-spread, not a duvet like people have today. The dressing table was quite neat, other than a bit of loose change spread on the top which amounted to a couple of pounds.

Gammon looked in the wardrobe. All his clothes looked like they had been purchased from charity shops. There were also a couple of pairs of down at heel shoes. Gammon had a quick root through coat pockets, but nothing seemed to be in the pockets.

He shut the wardrobe doors then noticed a book two thirds open on the bedside table. Gammon turned it over. It was a book written by Dr Virgil Grezny. The title was 'The Cancer Cure'.

Inside Grezny had written 'To all my followers. One day people will listen, and the greedy pharmaceutical companies will be taken to task as you know, and I know the cure'.

Gammon sat on the bed reading it when Smarty came in.

"Bloody hell, we got time to read now, detective?"

"Very funny Dave, I reckon we have our killer mate."

He threw Dave the book.

"Blimey, it says here that sodium hypochlorite will kill cancer cells, once they understand why everyone reacts different to it. That's Bleach John isn't it? I remember Wally educating us at a meeting."

"Spot on Dave, anything in the cellar?"

"No, nothing John."

"Ok, let's check the other rooms."

Gammon took the room on the left and Smarty the one on the right as they left Sower's bedroom.

THE CURE

"John, quick take a look at this."

Gammon shot across to Smarty. On the wall was a shelf with a bottle of bleach on it. There was a table set up with a bunsen burner, the type you used at school. There was a picture of poor Jessie Toppin. She had her mouth taped and she was tied to an old chair. On the wall were newspaper cuttings from his previous trial and some pictures of him and his girlfriend Jackie Bush smiling before they went into caught.

"This was one mixed up dude, John."

"You can say that again Dave. Just glad the bastard has killed himself, Dave."

"Ok, I have seen enough tell Wally to take a look at this room and Sower's bedroom for any clues on the other girls."

"Ok, John."

239

"When you have done that, let's
get back to Bixton and set the
meeting up in the incident room for
9.30am. Take your time mate, I need
a quick chat with Carl first."

Gammon went out of the house
feeling pleased, it looked like the
case was now done. His words to
Dirk were correct. He thought how
in these cases you get nothing for
ages then suddenly it falls into place.

Carl was sitting outside in his car
and John got in the passenger seat.
Carl's eyes were red and swollen,
and he was in a real mess.

"Look lad, for what it's worth, let
it go."

"I love her, John."

"If you love her, let it go. For the
protection people to have reacted so
quickly they must have intelligence
that she is still in danger, and I am
guessing they told her. She sees that

by leaving she saves you and any of your friends from being in danger."

"I'm not bothered about all that, John. I would have protected her."

"Look, why don't you take a week off and try and get your head correct mate. It looks like we have found the serial killer, so we should be able to cope without you for a week."

"Are you sure John? I'm not sure I could face people feeling like this."

"Not a problem, Carl. Right, I best get back with Smarty. See you in a week. You have my mobile if you need me."

"Thanks John, I really appreciate your kindness."

John left Carl and he and Smarty drove back to Bixton.

Gammon's first job was to talk to DCI Dirk. Although he was on holiday John was sure it would make his day. As expected Dirk repeated his and John's conversation and gave John a lot of praise.

"Sir, this job is 80 percent luck, you always need a break. Just to let you know, I let DI Milton have a week off. He has one or two family problems, and with this looking good I thought that you would be ok with it?"

"Not a problem John, thanks for keeping me up to speed."

"Well I should have more tomorrow, but I will drop you a report by e-mail."

"Great John, I can get e-mails ok."

"Ok Sir, enjoy your holiday," and Gammon rang off.

It was now 5.40pm so Gammon called it a night. It had been a good day. Hopefully tomorrow would confirm they had the right man for these murders once Wally had worked his magic.

There was only one place to go after such a good day and that was the Spinning Jenny. John wandered in and Kev was in his usual place reading his Racing Post.

"Pedigree, John?"

"Yes please, mate."

"You look pleased with yourself. Mind, you would be, we saw your car on the car park when we got back at midnight."

"Oh yeah, sat talking with Anouska."

"You must think I am as green as a cabbage, lad."

John smiled.

"No, just a cup of coffee and a chat. I left about 1.30am."

"No, you bloody didn't Mr Gammon," came a voice from the corridor.

"It was more like 5.00am because I got up for a glass of water and saw you pull of the car park."

John blushed a bit but then he always did when Doreen caught him out.

"Just going to say one thing. I know it's nothing to do with me and Kev knows my feelings on this. Just be careful with that one."

Doreen set off back to the kitchen.

"Do you and Doreen not agree, Kev?"

"Anouska is good for trade John, so no, I don't agree with her mate."

"I heard that," came a voice from the corridor.

Kev gestured for John to go to the end of the bar, furthest away from the corridor.

THE CURE

"Are you working tonight, mate?"

"Yes, Anouska has gone with Joni and Tracey to see Grease at Bixton Opera House, so I said I would work mate. How's Steve, John."

"Not heard anything today, and to be honest not had much time with work being so busy."

"Are you any nearer catching that bloody bleach nutcase?"

"Watch this space, Kev."

Around 8.00pm Jack and Bob came in. Bob was full of it.

"Have you two heard this one?"

"Tell them Bob. He's got new material now he has been to see that comedian the other night, lads."

"Do you have to, Bob?"

"I certainly do Kev, and I know you love my jokes."

Kev walked back up the bar to get Jack Etchings a pint of lager, shaking his head as he went up the bar to the pump.

"This guy walks into a pub with a giraffe. The giraffe had to bend his neck to fit in. He says to the landlord, a pint of bitter for me and a double brandy for the giraffe. The landlord looks at him but decides to serve them both. Anyway, the guy takes a sip of his beer then gets on a bar stool and the giraffe downs the double brandy. It affects him straight away and he falls over. The bar was quite busy so people had to climb over the giraffe. Eventually the man finishes his pint, puts his coat on and shouts goodnight to the landlord who is at the top of the bar serving. He comes running down, and says hang on mate, you can't leave that lying there. The man says it isn't a lion it's a giraffe."

THE CURE

John almost dropped his pint laughing, but Kev kept stony faced.

"Do me a favour Bob, keep the jokes for talentless night will you.

"You love them really, Kev."

"I bloody don't."

"Somebody said you were trying out a new barmaid the other night. Is it Gary Lewis's girlfriend?"

"Yes Jack, her name's Jane Halzimmer."

"Nice lass, wasn't her dad a German prisoner of war?"

"No that was her bloody grandad, Bob."

"She lives in Dilley Dale, so not far away and seems flexible on the hours."

By 9.00pm they arrived. Shelley, Cheryl, Sheba and Phil Sterndale who had picked the girls up. Carol Lestar and her Mum Freda had come in and sat at their favourite seat by the fire.

"Glad you are in John. I would have phoned you but didn't have your number, and Sheba was at badminton with this crazy lot."

"Why? What was up mate?"

"Nothing, other than I have had ITV and BBC camera crews at my house filming and asking questions. Was he the serial killer, John?"

"Why do you say that?"

"Well they said it was they were knocking on doors offering a hundred quid to anybody that had a picture of him."

Bugger, John thought.

"It's too early in the investigation, Phil."

"Well I am on the telly on News at Ten, they told me."

"Have you got a telly?"

THE CURE

Kev nipped out to one of the empty guest rooms and brought back a twenty three inch flat screen with a portable aerial.

"Not sure how good it will be with the portable aerial, Phil."

Phil set it up and the picture wasn't too bad. Jack got a round in and they all gathered round the telly for Phil's big night.

Eventually the new reader said they had breaking news from early today. The so called Guardian of the Bone Factory, the serial killer who had been administering bleach to his victims, had been found hung today in his garage by a local log salesman.

Over to Alistair Griffin.

"Phil was standing outside his house talking to Griffin. Phil explained what he had found, but did say he didn't know anything about the on-going police investigation.

The picture then cut to DCI Dirk
which shocked John.

"How the hell did they find him on
holiday?"

"DCI Dirk, very good of you to
talk to us tonight with you being on
holiday. We would like a comment
on the great news that your force
have got the serial killer?"

"Well I am not one to be looking
for glory, but my DI, John Gammon
and I have done a great job. Myself
and DI Gammon spoke a couple of
days ago and I mentioned that this
man was of great interest to me, so I
was pleased to be proved correct."

"You appear to have changed the
Bixton force, DCI Dirk."

John could see they were playing
to Dirk's ego and Dirk loved it.

"Well I have made quite a few
changes in the work ethic, and I
knew we were close before I left for

my holiday. Call it copper's intuition but the result tells you everything."

"Could I ask you a question, DCI Dirk?"

"Please feel free, we serve the public."

"DI Gammon has been involved in quite a few high profile cases. Word is that he isn't good with the media, and his way of getting results is too maverick for people higher up the food chain. Am I correct?"

"Well I have found DI Gammon to be a good detective, but he does have a few rough edges. I am sure if I keep polishing him, his diamond abilities will come through."

"Thank you for that DCI Dirk. Enjoy the rest of your holiday. The Peak District public can sleep tonight."

John was seething. They didn't even know until tomorrow if Sowers had killed the first victim Jessie Toppin. Never mind the last victim Mandy Bellows, and there he was taking the credit for a completed job.

"What you having to drink, rough diamond?" Bob said.

"Bollocks Bob."

"He was bloody full of himself mate. No credit to you and the rest of the team as such, but I guess that's gaffers for you, John. I am only joking mate, we all know how hard you work, John."

"Aye we do that, John lad."

"Thanks Jack, it's just so bloody annoying."

"Forget it John, let's have a beer. My old dad used to say never look for medals, because if you get them they bloody hurt when they pull them off."

"Seemed like a wise man, your dad Phil."

THE CURE

"He certainly was, Cheryl."

They carried on drinking until all most midnight then left and went their separate ways. John had a quick Jameson's before climbing into bed, still annoyed at the comments from Dirk. It wasn't so much the glory, but what if this guy hadn't killed all the victims.

John didn't sleep well and was at work for 8.00pm.

"Morning Sir."

"Good morning. Sergeant Beeney, everything ok last night?"

"Here? Oh yes Sir, but did you see the 10.00pm news?"

"I'm afraid I did Sergeant, and I don't want to discuss it thanks."

Gammon climbed the stairs and grabbed a cup of dishwater coffee before standing at his office window looking over to Losehill.

At 8.30am Steve rang.

"Can you do me a favour mate?"

"If I can Bud, what is it?"

"I need to get a new motor and fancy a Porsche Cayan. I have seen one in Halifax. Any chance of a lift to go and have a look Saturday?"

"Of course mate. I'll pick you up. I will see you in the week anyway."

Steve seemed ok John thought. He just needed to keep Lund's involvement away from Steve, or he could end up with another situation like he had with his brother Adam.

John made his way down to the incident room. Everyone was in and as usual the banter started.

"Come on rough diamond. Anyone seen the polish," shouted DI Lee.

"Alright, alright, you have had your fun. Now let's get down to business."

"What have we got, Wally?"

THE CURE

"Ok, David Sowers did commit suicide, but I am not convinced he meant to."

"Why Wally?"

"I think this was a cry for help. When Mr Sterndale found him he had not been dead very long, in fact I would say seconds."

"Well that fits in with the instruction to drop the logs off in the garage."

"Second thing, the rope was actually too long to break the neck, he choked to death. The chair was almost within reach, and my guess was he tried to get back on it when he realised time was running out."

"The picture of the girl, what evidence have you she had been at the house, Wally?

"Absolutely none, but we did find some green overalls with his and the lady in question's DNA on them, so they had been in contact John."

"Did you find anything that could incriminate Sowers to the murders?"

"Yes, we did. We found a bottle of sodium hydroxide. This had the girl's DNA on the mouth of the bottle, and his DNA and fingerprints on the bottle."

"Finally John, we found what appeared to be a suicide note for some reason bizarrely put it in the bread bin. Don't ask me why?"

"What did it say?"

It said, 'My darling Jackie, I have tried so hard for you and I believe we were so close, but now it doesn't matter' and it was signed 'David'."

"Is that it, Wally?"

"Yes, John."

"Thanks again to you and your team for a great job again."

THE CURE

The room clapped as Wally went back to his seat.

"Ok, picking up on the letter, what did he mean by 'we' do you think?

"Guessing he must mean Jackie Bush?"

"But I thought that was over long ago. Didn't she do an article in The News Of The World saying she should never have been convicted? Sowers was a control freak and she thought she was drinking bleach like the rest?"

"Yeah, I remember that, DI Lee."

"Maybe it was just a front, but whichever way DS Yap and myself are off to Hartlepool to question Jackie Bush first thing in the morning."

Yap was quite pleased that he had been chosen. He had a lot of respect for Gammon and looked up to him.

Gammon left the incident room to be told a reporter from the Peakland View was in his office waiting for him. Gammon was furious.

"Don't ever put anybody in my office again, Beeney."

He said he had a 9.00am meeting with you, Sir."

"Use your bloody head man. He is a reporter sniffing a story and you put him in my office with all my sensitive information. You are a clown, Beeney," and Gammon shot up the stairs to his office.

He opened the door to find two reporters, a man and a woman. One had also sneaked past Beeney.

"What the hell do you two want?"

"Not a nice greeting, DI Gammon."

Gammon noticed the woman scribbling on her pad. You have no right to be here, we have no meeting arranged. Your kind officer sent us up here. Gammon was at exploding point with Beeney to have put him and the station in this position.

"So, you are confident we can all rest in our beds that the so called Guardian of the Bone Factory is now under arrest?"

Gammon knew whatever he said that this idiot would blow it all out of proportion.

"DC I Dirk seems to have got the station organised and running smoothly. Would you say he was a good acquisition for the station?"

"My personal thoughts on fellow officers are exactly that, so I have no comment to make."

Gammon knew to throw them out with nothing would mean they would make some story up.

"Are you not a little miffed that you were looked over for the DCI

job here at Bixton? They brought
this highly professional guy in which
in all honesty looks like a good
appointment, DI Gammon?"

"I don't make decisions. I am here
to serve the people of the Peak
District to the best of my abilities,
and my peers make those decisions."

The reporters knew they had
Gammon on the ropes and one off
the cuff remark could cause him
major embarrassment.

"I was a reporter when you arrived
for your first case, the prostitutes'
murders, and wasn't that something
to do with your brother who went on
to commit an atrocity in the Drovers
Arms pub?"

"I don't really think this has
anything to do with the case you
have supposedly come to talk to me
about. Seeing that you are here

without an appointment I would like you to leave as I am very busy."

The two reporters got up without a word and left. Gammon called Beeney to his office.

"Sergeant, you are lucky that I don't send your ass back to traffic. If you ever pull a stunt like that again that will be the consequence. Do I make myself crystal clear, Sergeant Beeney?"

"Yes Sir, I am very sorry, it won't happen again."

"Right, send DS Yap to my office."

"Ok Sir," and Beeney left. Yap arrived.

"Come in Ian. Tomorrow morning we will need to leave at 5.45am from here at Bixton. The woman we are going to see lives at 16 Grange Sands Terrace in Hartlepool. If we are there for 8.00am we will have a

good chance of catching her in case
she goes to work."

"Good thinking, Sir. That's fine,
do you want me to drive?"

"You might as well, Ian."

THE CURE

CHAPTER SIX

The following day Gammon arrived at Bixton and DS Yap was waiting.

"Plugged the postcode in Sir, so we are all set."

They arrived at Jackie Bush's address and Gammon knocked on the door. It was a terrace of Coronation Street type houses. There was no answer. Eventually a lady from next door popped her head out of an upstairs window.

"What do you want, Mister?"

"Oh, hello. I am DI John Gammon, and this is DS Yap. Is the lady of the house in?"

"Who, Jackie?"

"Yes, Jackie Bush."

"She won't be back."

"What do you mean?"

"Hang on, I'll come down to you."

The woman in her early forties
came down. She was heavily made
up but had like a smock you see
factory girls wearing. She had a head
scarf on and what looked like hair
curlers. She stood on the front step
with a cigarette in one hand whilst
chewing gum.

"So, what did you want with
Jackie?"

"Did she have any male visitors
lately, do you know?"

"You don't know she is dead, do
you?"

"What?"

"Yes, she died about four days
ago. Her funeral is next week."

"Before she died, did she have any
visitors?"

"She knew she hadn't got long, so
she told me her friend would be
coming to see her for a couple of
days."

THE CURE

"Did she say a name?"

"Yes, ugh David I think."

"What about a surname?"

"Sowers, I think."

"Ok, well thank you."

"So what had she done?"

"Oh, nothing, just had a couple of questions for her."

Gammon and Yap left.

"Chances are she has bleach in her body, and the letter was him saying he had one last try doing what they both believed all those years ago."

Gammon phoned Hartlepool police and told them he needed a copy of the post mortem e-mailed onto him. It wasn't going to make any difference now they were both dead, but Gammon liked a tidy end to things.

It was almost 3.30pm when they landed back at Bixton and Gammon checked his e-mails as soon as he got back. Jackie Bush's post mortem picked up on the bleach, but they had put it down to her being delirious at the end. Gammon was pretty sure that Sowers had something to do with it. But there was no point using police resources looking in the house for clues to see if he did the deed as he was dead.

Gammon finished of the report on the two murdered brothers, putting it down to a case of drug suppliers falling out.

The deaths of Jo and Leah Marie he placed firmly at the door of the Gabble brothers, Piers and Leroy. He omitted his thoughts about Lund knowing that if Steve got whiff he would kill Lund, or at least try. Gammon was saving that deed he for himself one day. John decided to give Steve a ring to see how he was, and to see if he wanted to meet him for a pint. Steve answered.

"John you ok?"

"Hi mate, yeah ok. Just wondered if you wanted a beer after work?"

"Yeah, that would be good, John."

"I'll pick you up about 6.00pm, Steve."

John thought he best start getting Steve back into reality after the awful time he had been through.

It was 6.10pm when John pulled up at Tracey Rodger's lodge. Steve was waiting at the door.

"Looking dapper, Mr Lineman."

"Thanks mate, Tracey took me into Ackbourne. I lost all my clothes in the fire."

"Have you heard when the insurance company will settle, Steve?"

"Yes mate, they say within six weeks. They think the value is going to be close to three million on the property, and also on top of that the life insurance to pay out."

John didn't comment. He could see Steve was quite shaken talking about the death of Jo and Leah Marie.

"Right where do you fancy, Steve?"

"Can you remember a pub called The Star in Puddle Dale?"

"Oh yeah, didn't you take the landlord's daughter out before you went in the Navy?"

"Certainly did. What was her name, it was dead posh, wasn't it?"

"Yeah John, her name was Imogen, Imogen Elliot. I read in the Bixton Post that she has taken over from her mum and dad."

"I haven't seen her for almost twenty years, mate."

THE CURE

"If I remember correctly she was quite a stunner, wasn't she?"

"Certainly was mate, we split because she didn't want me to go in the Navy."

"Come on then. It's only fifteen minutes from here, Steve."

It was a typically drizzly night and quite misty as they pulled into the car park of the Star Inn. John noticed that some wag had spray painted in the pub sign 'SUPER' to make the word Super star.

"Let's hope it lives up to its name, eh mate."

The front door looked about two hundred years old. They entered the snug there were three old blokes playing dominoes, and a lady behind the bar. The barmaid recognised Steve immediately.

"Bloody hell, Steve Lineman."

Although Imogen had got older she was still a good looking lass and dressed very well.

"It must be all of twenty years Steve. How are you?"

"Oh, ok I guess. I read in the Bixton Post you had took the pub on."

"Yes, I was actually living in Milan. I was a fashion designer for Roland Bell."

John knew straight away that Roland Bell was a really famous name in the fashion industry, but he could tell Steve didn't have a clue who she was talking about.

"You remember Porky Gammon, don't you Imogen?"

"Yes, didn't you join the police?"

"Yeah, he is a Detective Inspector now at Bixton."

THE CURE

"Really, well done. You let me get you both a drink and we can have a chinwag."

"What bitters have you got, Imogen?"

"I'm afraid only Old Nelly. My mum and dad ran stocks down because they didn't think I wanted the pub. So, this being my first week I am playing catch up."

"Two of them then please Imogen, and take one yourself."

"Very good of you John. Sit down over there and I'll come and sit with you for five minutes."

They sat down and Imogen came over. John could see the designer clothes. The three of them sat talking.

"So, is there a Mr Imogen?"

"No Steve, I never married but concentrated on my career."

Luckily she didn't ask Steve but while Steve was at the toilet John gave her a potted history of what happened.

By 8.50pm Imogen had to get back behind the bar as the pub had filled up. They decided to finish their drink and have one in Toad Holes at the Wobbly Man. They were just about to leave when a guy shouted, "How are you John?"

John looked over and saw Brian Lund with two blonde haired girls. John stared at him and told Steve to hurry up.

Once in the car Steve asked who the guy was.

"Brian Lund, mate."

"What? I thought he was dead."

"So did I Steve, it's a long complicated story."

THE CURE

"He must have lost five stones. I don't think I would have recognised him."

John heard Steve's words, but he was quite sure he would never forget Lund, and his mate wouldn't if he knew what he had done.

"What did you think of Imogen, John?"

"Yes, seems like a nice girl, well woman I guess, and sounds like she did well for herself."

"Funny how she remembered me, mate."

"Well you haven't changed that much, Steve."

"What you mean I am still that debonair good-looking guy you knew all those years ago, mate?"

"Yeah, something like that."

It was good to see Steve having a bit of banter.

They arrived at the Wobbly Man and Joni was behind the bar.

"Hey John, how are you?"

"Steve, so sorry for your tragedy and loss."

"Thanks Joni, can we have two pints of Muck-duster please."

Joni realised he didn't want to talk about what had happened.

"So, what brings you two to Toad Holes?"

"Just having a ride round. We have just been up to Puddle Dale and called at the Star."

"Oh, I saw they have a new owner, don't they?"

"Yes, Imogen Elliot bought it off her parents. She is an old flame of Steve's."

"Quite a small world, hey Steve."

"Yeah, funny how life dishes things out."

THE CURE

The Wobbly was quite busy, so they just had the one and decided to finish off at the Spinning Jenny.

Kev was customer side of the bar and Anouska was showing the new girl, Jane Halzimmer, the ropes.

"Hey lovely to see you lad," Kev said putting his arms round Steve in a bear hug. That was Kev, he was quite demonstrative if he liked you.

They had a couple more and told Kev where they had been.

"We looked at buying the Star when we first came round here, but it didn't have the scope like the Spinning Jenny, with the accommodation and camping, so we didn't bother. Who has got it now? Old Arthur Elliot and his wife have run that for some years."

"His daughter Kev, Imogen."

"Really, I heard she was a top fashion designer abroad somewhere. Done very well for herself they say."

"Yes mate, that's her. She was working in Milan but has given it all up to carry on the tradition of the Elliot's running The Star. She will have some work on, Steve. They don't even have a darts and domino team anymore."

"Think she has money to throw at it, Kev. She has bought all the outbuildings of Bonsa Farm and intends turning them into accommodation. It's right on the Limestone Way."

"Sounds like she has her head screwed on, John."

"I agree mate."

"Right, we are calling it a night Kev. I've got a lot on at the minute."

THE CURE

"Alright lads, go careful and lovely to see you Steve. I will tell Doreen you popped in."

John dropped Steve off and they decided to go to look at the car on Saturday morning. John said he would see him at 10.00am.

On the way back John knew he had been a bit quiet. He had been surprised to see Lund in the Star. Was he taunting me he thought?

The following day John was up bright and early. He showered, got changed and then sat in the garden with a bacon sandwich and a strong black coffee. It was warm, and John loved seeing the squirrels bobbing about and the rest of the wildlife. John savoured his bacon sandwich and coffee for a good hour before setting off to pick Steve up. When he arrived at the Lodge, Steve came out

and said he had seen a nicer Porsche
Cayan in Retford near Nottingham.

"Not a problem mate, let's go
buying," and John laughed.

"I know its early days mate, but
what are you going to do with the
house?"

"I know what I want to do. I am
going to rebuild it exactly as Jo had
it and I am going to call it Joleah
Country House, John."

John wasn't sure that was a good
idea, but didn't say. At least his mate
was moving forward and it would
take his mind off all the stuff and the
people involved.

"Been thinking as well, mate. Do
you fancy a week away
somewhere?"

"Where, Steve?"

"What about the West coast of
Scotland? We could drive up and
stay a night in Edinburgh, then carry

on up to one of those remote villages."

"Sounds good to me, mate."

"Well I would like to do it before the money comes through to start rebuilding the house, mate."

"I'm good with that. It's quiet at work at the minute, but things can change."

"Just say the word."

"I tell you what Steve, I'll have a look on the internet tomorrow and see if I can find a little village with a nice pub, and some walks. What do you reckon?"

"Ok with the first bit, but don't want twenty flippin mile walks every day, Porky."

"No, I was thinking more of a stroll between village pubs, Mr Lineman."

"Sort it then, mate."

"I will, Steve."

They arrived at M and K Car Sales. The first impression was good, they sold all prestige cars. John let Steve talk to the sales guy about the Porsche Cayan he liked, and John had a wander round the car lot.

John spotted a black Mercedes SLK with cream leather interior and all the trimmings. He quite fancied it, but Steve was shouting him over to look at the Porsche with him. John could tell that it didn't matter what the salesmen said, or to that mind John, Steve had his heart set on this vehicle. The guy never had such an easy sale. Thirty seven thousand, seven hundred and fifty pounds and Steve didn't try to knock him down, he wanted it that bad.

With the deal done John followed Steve back home. The Porsche was a beast of a car. When they arrived at the Lodge Steve said he would do

THE CURE

the drive up to Scotland while the Porsche was in warranty.

The following morning John settled down a coffee and a slice of toast. With his laptop he started looking for coastal cottages on the West coast. After ten minutes he came across a village called Lockleish with a small two bed roomed cottage. The village had a small pub and a small fishing boat that did three hour fishing trips, which John thought would be good. The next village, Doone, was about three miles walk, so ideal he thought. He rang Steve and they agreed they would go for it the week after next. So John booked it.

The rest of the day he tidied the garden and did a small walk into Hittington. One of the pubs did good Sunday lunches so he popped in there. The Bear in the Lane was an old pub built around 1760. It still had flag floors and oak beams everywhere. The couple that ran it had done so for about eighteen years, Sam and Heather Dolan. The pub had a great reputation for Sunday lunches.

John settled down with a pint of Crooked Shep bitter and a beautiful Sunday lunch. He could hardly walk when he paid the bill to leave, he was that full.

On the way out he bumped into Phil Sterndale and Sheba. Sheba seemed really happy. They said they had done a short walk with Phil's dog Gamble.

"That's a strange name for a dog Phil, why Gamble?"

"I got her from a rescue and it's always a gamble what you might get.

THE CURE

So, I called her Gamble for that reason."

"Are you coming back in for a pint, mate?"

"No, I best get back Phil, don't think I could drink a pint anyway."

"Oh, have you had one of Heather's home-made Bear in the Lane Sunday lunches? To die for, aren't they John?"

"They certainly are."

John said goodbye and left Phil, Sheba and Gamble. He headed back up the village, across three open fields and up two sets of steps. That reminded him of the days he and Adam played Cowboys and Indians using the steps and fence as a fort.

John arrived back at his cottage at almost 8.00pm feeling shattered. He quickly showered and got into bed.

The following day at the station
DCI Dirk was back off holiday, and
Sergeant Beeney informed John that
he was holding a meeting at 9.30am
in the incident room.

John followed DI Scooper down
the stairs to the meeting.

"What's this about, John? How
great he was at catching the bleach
guy, and how dumb we all were until
he came to pulls us up by our
bootlaces?"

"Don't know Sandra, something
like that I bet."

The room was full when DCI Dirk
came in slightly bronzed from his
break abroad.

"Good morning. I just wanted to
thank you for your gallant efforts in
closing the self-styled Bone Factory
murderer. Sometimes in policing you
need a break, and we got one. The
hierarchy are very pleased, and as I

said to them, it's testament to the hard working committed officers under my command."

Smarty turned to Milton and whispered bullshit.

"Yes, DI Smarty did you want to say anything?"

"Sorry Sir, got a tickle in my throat."

The rest of the officers laughed. Deep down Dirk knew he had taken the glory without doing anything to warrant it.

"So, life is back to normal. I think we can safely shut this case." Gammon had heard enough.

"Do you think that's wise, Sir. I mean we haven't really got anything concrete on Sowers with regard to the other victims."

"It's a numbers game, and the years you have been in the force I would have thought you, of all people, would know that we mopped up four murders by Sowers, and the double murder of your friend and her daughter by those low-lifes found on the moor. So, with that in mind I have arranged a few sandwiches and drinks on me after work tonight. All welcome. I am told this is what you do here in Bixton when you have some success."

They all clapped but John wasn't sure Dirk was right. He had no choice but to go along with it.

The meeting finished, and Dirk asked Gammon to stop behind.

"You don't seem convinced, Gammon?"

"I am with you Sir, but I just don't want us to get it wrong. I was involved in arresting a man a couple of years back, and the case was thrown out of court. It has always left a bad taste in my mouth."

THE CURE

"Oh yes, the Alison case. Well don't worry Gammon, I don't make big mistakes like that."

If only he knew who killed the scumbags Gammon thought.

Gammon did his paperwork all day and dropped in his holiday request Dirk could hardly knock it back as he had just had a week off, and the cases were put to bed so there was no problem.

"Are you going John? It's 5.30pm, they will all be at the Spinning Jenny now."

"Yeah, coming Sandra."

"It's just fell right for me John. Mum and Rosie have gone to see Mum's gardener who is in hospital. He has worked for her for over forty five years and he had a bad stroke two days ago. He thinks the world of Rosie, so Mum thought it might cheer him up if she took Rosie. Then they are calling at McDonalds for a happy meal.

"I'll see you up there, John."

Gammon finished off and shut down his laptop. He arrived at the Spinning Jenny feeling unsure. John always liked these get-togethers with his colleagues, but this didn't feel right. It was like the other murdered girls had been forgotten.

"Pedigree John?"

"Oh, yes please Sir."

To be fair to DCI Dirk, he actually believed the hype and was trying to get the whole station to enjoy the moment.

John stood with Dave Smarty and Sandra Scooper. By 7.00pm Dave was quite drunk and Sandra was also quite giggly.

"What's up John? Has he stolen your thunder?"

THE CURE

"No, not at all Sandra. I am just not sure Sowers killed all our victims."

"You have to say though John, that it looks pretty convincing," Dave said with quite slurred speech.

DCI Dirk by now was also quite merry. He shouted, "Order."

He wanted to make a speech. Dirk stood on a stool.

"I propose a toast to all my colleagues, a wonderful team of detectives and police officers. I would like to think my policing methods, that you all bought into, are now paying dividends. Your station has had numerous DCI's which doesn't help moral, and I am sure there were some good and some bad in there. DI Gammon included, but you will all have your own thoughts on that. So, it leaves no more to say other than cheers, enjoy the night."

John felt furious inside. Was he
saying he had been a bad DCI? With
Sandra tipsy and Dave being put in a
taxi he nipped to the toilet. On the
way back DI Milton spoke with him.

"John, you are the best DCI the
station ever had. This bullshit is
beyond me, and you would get my
vote all day every day, mate. I will
tell you something else, that goes for
the whole station."

"Thanks Carl, that means a lot."

He didn't want to stay talking to
Carl. With the Beth thing so raw he
knew the conversation would
eventually get back to Beth. He
thanked Carl and went back to
Sandra.

Sandra was quite wobbly, and she
whispered in John's ear, "Can I stop
with you tonight?"

It seemed like it was going from a
crap night to quite a good one. John

gave her a key to the cottage and said she should go in a taxi. He would follow in half an hour so that they didn't raise suspicion.

It was 9.40pm when he left the pub. Most of them had left so John saw his opportunity. He climbed the back steps to his car just as Anouska was coming out of her room.

"Oh, hi Anouska, how are you?"

"Yes ok, thank you."

She looked very pale under the outside light. John could see she didn't want to talk so he said goodnight and drove home.

The door to the cottage was ajar so he entered almost falling over a black pair of stiletto heels and a coat of Sandra's on the floor. John climbed the stairs and Sandra was in his bed. She smiled at him. She still had her underwear on so looked quite seductive. John stripped off and climbed into bed with her. For almost an hour they pleasured each other's bodies before finally making love. It had seemed so long, and John and Sandra never made lust, it always felt like love.

Finally exhausted Sandra lay her head on John's chest and was soon asleep. John lay there for almost two hours thinking about the case and DCI Dirk and what he had implied.

The last time John looked at his bedside clock it was 3.17am so when his alarm went off at 7.15am it startled both of them.

"Oh, hell John. I need to get my car and get home to get some fresh clothes."

They both quickly got dressed and John took Sandra for her car at the Spinning Jenny. He returned, showered, shaved and changed and headed in to work, calling at Beryl's

THE CURE

Baps for a doorstep bacon butty to go with a strong black coffee. John pulled up by Monkdale to admire the tremendous view and eat his sandwich. It was a bit out of his way, but he was early anyway so five minutes didn't matter.

Looking towards the magnificent viaduct where the steam trains had run until Doctor Beeching's axe fell in the early nineteen sixties. John's mum often used to talk about the fabulous viaduct at Monkdale. When she was a little girl her mum and dad would take her to watch the steam trains head across the viaduct going to Manchester.

With his sandwich and coffee finished John headed for Bixton.

"Morning, Sergeant Beeney, everything ok last night?"

"Nothing to report, Sir. Oh, other than DS Magic won't be in. He said he has got the flu."

"More like he is bloody hungover, the amount of Guinness he consumed last night, Sergeant."

Gammon climbed the stairs passing DCI Dirk.

"Good morning, John."

"Good morning, Sir."

"Did you enjoy our little forage last night?"

Gammon could hardly say no.

"Oh, yes Sir."

"Great result for Bixton John, great result," and he left Gammon with his mouth open as he skipped down the stairs.

Gammon grabbed a coffee and went to his desk. DI Scooper put her head round the door.

"Thanks for the lift John. Oh and the other bits."

THE CURE

Gammon blushed, and Sandra closed the door.

Gammon still had his mind on the other suspects as he wasn't convinced that Dirk had got this one right.

Gammon wrote on his pad 'Mark Block' and he underlined it two or three times. He then wrote 'Andrew Firm' and finally 'Andrew Gilbon' and again he underlined Gilbon's name two or three times.

Gammon was pondering. What had he missed? He wrote 'Block junior doctor Micklock'. He then wrote 'would have known Helen Firm and Jessie Toppin both junior nurses'.

'Andrew Firm married to Helen Firm but only in name, no love lost there' he wrote.

'The victim number one: Jessie Topping girlfriend of Mark Block

found by the café in the park at
Micklock.'

Gammon scribbled down' Block
knew two of the dead women Jessie
Toppin and Helen Firm'.

'Andrew Firm, motive possible
jealousy he and his wife were not
getting on' but then Gammon wrote
'weakest suspect'.

'Andrew Gilbon, nasty piece of
work. Works where Maga Wuxi
studied. DNA found on her handbag
excuse was he just picked it up'.
Gammon wrote 'feasible'. He then
wrote 'big suspect'.

Gammon stood staring out of his
office window towards Losehill
pondering if he should carry on the
investigation, chancing the wrath of
DCI Dirk, or just let sleeping dog's
lye. The problem he had now was he
was wrestling with his conscience.
He really didn't want the murder of

the two brothers bringing up again so knew he had to tread carefully with DCI Dirk.

John phoned Steve to tell him the holiday was on.

"Are you out tonight mate?"

"No, but thanks for asking John. Tracey is cooking a stew and dumplings and I said I would watch a film. Think she is feeling a bit down and I'm not one hundred percent mate, but looking forward to Scotland, and thanks for the thought."

Gammon decided to speak to Wally about his thoughts, so he popped down to forensics. Wally's office was always clean, tidy and well organised. It was like he never went in, but that was Wally, always tidy and efficient.

"Afternoon Mr Gammon, on to what do we owe the pleasure of the

Peak District's answer to Sherlock Holmes?"

"Very funny Wally, just after your opinion."

"Only joking mate, just rare we ever see any of you detective lads down here."

Gammon started to explain his misgivings with Sowers being blamed for all the murders.

"Well John, I gave you all the evidence we could find, and as much as I don't like how Dirk as taken the credit, I think he is possibly right mate."

"Well that will do for me mate, you are very rarely wrong."

"Right, well let me get on," and Wally laughed as he walked away.

John returned to his office and as he stood staring at Losehill DS Yap came in.

THE CURE

"Excuse me, Sir. I have a concern."

"What is it, Ian?"

"This might sound crazy, but I don't agree with DCI Dirk about Sowers killing all those girls."

"What makes you think that?"

"I think we have come to the conclusion too quickly, Sir."

"Well first things first, if it's of any interest to you Ian, I think the same way. But before we go any further, this must not get out for either of us. At best if DCI Dirk isn't wrong and we are, we will both be directing traffic. Are we clear DS Yap?"

"Yes Sir, but how do we prove we are right?"

"Tomorrow we find a way. I intend on somehow getting DNA from Mark Block and Andrew Gilbon."

"Great Sir, I can't wait."

"Ok, I will see you in the morning, Ian."

Yap left Gammon's office and he shut down his laptop and called it a night. John drove straight home. Phyllis Swan had made him pasta carbonara that just needed reheating.

He set the microwave for three minutes and was just about to pour a glass of red wine when his phone rang. It was Anouska, she was crying.

"Anouska, what's a matter?"

"We need to talk John," she said in broken English.

"Can it wait?"

Anouska became quite irate.

"No, it can't wait, John Gammon. Pick me up, I will be on the car park at 7.30pm. It's my night off, don't not turn up," and the phone call ended.

THE CURE

John was intrigued so he quickly showered and changed and set off for the Spinning Jenny. It was a miserable night as John's car turned into the car park lighting up the slender figure of Anouska waiting for him.

"What's with the secrecy, Anouska?" She was crying as she climbed in the car.

"It's a mess, such a bloody mess."

"What is Anouska? You aren't making sense, have you lost your job?"

"Not yet."

"What do you mean, not yet? What's happened?"

That's when Anouska blurted out, "I'm pregnant. It's yours John."

Anouska just glared back at him with an uncompromising look.

"I don't know what to say, Anouska."

"Well, I didn't expect you to be pleased, but don't ask me if I am going to have an abortion? Because that isn't going to happen, my faith won't allow it, and I don't believe in it anyway."

John was lost for words.

"Don't worry, I don't want anything from you, but I thought you should know. I have decided to go home to be with my family."

"Are you staying there?"

"Yes, so nothing will affect your life. You don't have to worry, I won't tell anyone and I won't be back, John."

"When are you leaving?"

"Hopefully in a couple of days."

"Look Anouska, I need to set up some kind of monthly fund for you and the baby."

"You don't have to do anything John, but if you wish to its only fair.

THE CURE

I will have a DNA test and I will send you pictures of the baby when it's born."

"I'm going now John, I will be in touch."

With that she kissed John and left him on the car park with his life in turmoil once again. John started the car and headed home. His appetite was spoilt, he turned to a bottle of Jameson's and sat by the log fire unsure of what to do. If this got out Saron would certainly not bother with him ever again. It was almost 2.30am and two thirds of a bottle of Jameson's had gone. Although now in bed John had a disturbed sleep.

As he drove into work he wished he hadn't arranged to go with Sergeant Yap to somehow get DNA from Block and Gilbon.

He arrived at the station feeling
lousy. Yap was waiting in the car-
park. Lucky for Gammon he didn't
have to go in the station and they
headed for Block's house on Beerly
Moor.

It was quite a bright morning as
they arrived at Poppy Mill. Block
was just pulling up at the same time.
Yap had said he thought a good way
to get DNA from both men was if
Gammon kept them talking while he
used their toilet. Gammon didn't
disagree he was feeling rough and
had more on his mind after the
previous night's news from
Anouska.

"Good morning, Mr Block."

Block looked shocked and nervous
to find the two officers at his house
so early.

"Yes, good morning, how can I
help you?"

THE CURE

"Well, you can certainly help us. Would you be willing to come to the station today and do a DNA test?"

DS Yap looked confused at Gammon. Block hesitated.

"What today?"

"Yes, if you don't mind, Mr Block."

"I have to say I feel this is an infringement of my rights."

"I am not making you do this. I thought you would want to help with your girlfriend being one of the victims, Mr Block."

Gammon could see he had Block looking like a scared rabbit in a car's headlights.

"Ok Mr Gammon, when you put it like that, I will pop down to the station about 2.00pm today when I have had some sleep. It's been a heavy night at the hospital."

"Thank you, Mr Block."

"Before you go, I thought this case was now closed?"

"A case is never closed when the supposed perpetrator isn't able to confirm or answer questions, Mr Block."

Gammon and Yap left Block on his doorstep.

"He seemed guilty as sin, Sir."

"Let's not jump to conclusions, Yap."

"I thought you wanted me to get some DNA from him?"

"I remembered DCI Dirk is in London the rest of this week taking the plaudits for solving the Peak District's crime epidemic."

"Come on, let's get over to Andrew Gilbon see if we can get DNA from him."

THE CURE

Gammon drove over to Dilley Dale to see Gilbon.

They knocked on his door but there was no answer, so they went around the back and knocked again. Gammon peered through the window that hadn't been cleaned in an eternity. He could see what looked like a woman on the kitchen floor.

"Kick the door in, DS Yap."

Two big shoulder efforts and they were with the girl on the kitchen floor. It was Jane Sharpe and she was convulsing but still alive.

"Yap, get an ambulance urgently."

On the floor by her side was a small bottle of sodium hypochlorite

Gammon quickly opened the fridge door. There was a container of milk inside. He got Yap to help him and he made her drink milk. She kept being sick, but that didn't matter it meant the milk was working. Just before the paramedics arrived she had stopped being sick which meant the milk had taken effect.

"Your quick thinking probably saved this lady's life, Mr Gammon. We will take her now to Micklock hospital and they will do a gastric lavage, which basically means she will have a tube put in her stomach and the contents washed out."

"Will she be ok?"

"Difficult to say, but the signs are good. Now we must get her to hospital."

Gammon turned to Yap, "Call the station. I want DI Smarty and Lee down here and I want forensics going all over the house. Leave nothing to chance, check the loft, in fact every area, Yap."

"Will do, Sir."

THE CURE

"I'm following the ambulance, so you get a lift back with Smarty when you are done."

Gammon followed the ambulance and sat waiting until eventually a nurse came out and said, "Jane is ok. She is sore but we don't think there will be any long term effects, DI Gammon. She will be on Stinton Ward in about five minutes, if you wish to speak with her."

"Thank you, nurse."

"No, thank you. Jane works the opposite shift to me and is a lovely girl."

Ten minutes later the nurses made Jane comfortable in a private wing of the hospital. Then they allowed Gammon in.

The nurse said, "Five minutes please, Mr Gammon. Jane may struggle for a few days with the soreness of her throat."

"Ok, thank you nurse."

"Jane, DI Gammon. Just a quick few questions. Did Gilbon do this to you?"

She nodded and pointed to a pen and pad, and indicated she wanted to write sooner than talk.

She started scribbling answers for Gammon.

"How long were you at the house?"

'Two days' she wrote. 'He grabbed me again at a bus stop after my shift. He said I would be the perfect student. I struggled but he had chloroform on a rag over my mouth.'

"How did you end up in the kitchen?"

'He kept me dozy and tied up the first day. Then when you found me he was making me drink what looked like grape fruit juice, and it tasted a bit like it too. I kept asking him why he was doing this to me?'

"What did he say?"

"He just laughed and said I shouldn't have hit him. He said I would live if I drank the solution. I was so scared, then I heard a banging on the door. I think he panicked. He hit me and said bitch, then went out of the back door locking it as he went.'

"Well thank you Jane. We will get this monster. I may need to speak with you again once you have built your strength up."

Jane nodded.

Gammon could do no more so headed back to Bixton. It was almost 5.00pm when he arrived at the station. He asked Sergeant Beeney if Block had been in for the DNA test.

"I believe so, Sir. I think Laura from forensics did it."

"Is she still here?"

"Yes, I think so, she usually says goodnight as she passes."

Gammon went straight to forensics. Laura was just putting her coat.

"Evening Sir, can I help you? John Walvin and the rest of the team are at a suspect's house."

"Yes. I know Laura. Did you get a DNA sample from a Mark Block?"

"Yes, Sir."

"Did it tell us anything?"

"To be honest, I have only been in the forensic team for three days, so Mr Walvin said he would sort when he got back."

"Ok Laura, thank you."

Gammon told Beeney that when Wally came back to get him to come and see him once he had checked out

THE CURE

Block's DNA. He wanted the result tonight whatever it took, and he would be in his office.

Gammon grabbed a coffee and set about his paperwork. It was now 6.10pm.

It was another three hours before a tired looking Wally came in his office.

"Good evening, hard task master."

"Hey Wally, how are you?"

"Knackered John, but I have some interesting DNA results. It's with probable certainty that Mark Block was the son of David Sowers."

Gammon punched the air.

"Well done Wally. Do you have a match for a mother?"

"Sorry mate no, nothing on the data-base."

"Well no problem, great job again. We have a warrant out for Andrew Gilbon, but he has disappeared at the minute. Do you fancy a quick pint, Wally?"

"Blimey no John, her indoors will kill me with the hours I am putting in. She already thinks I am just the lodger," and he laughed.

"Ok mate, well thanks again."

Gammon nipped back to his office shut down his laptop and said goodnight to Di Trimble who had just come on for her shift.

John didn't want to go to the Spinning Jenny just yet. He thought he would leave it until Anouska left. He knew it was a bit of cowardice on his part, but the last thing he wanted was Carol Lestar or somebody getting wind of Anouska's pregnancy and Saron finding out.

He decided to call for a quick drink at the Tow'd Man. He pulled into the car park and made his way into the pub. There were a couple of local lads throwing darts, six walkers and Donna behind the bar.

"Hey John, Saron isn't in tonight. She has gone out with Doreen from the Spinning Jenny, some kind of landlady's ball in Derby."

"Why didn't you go?"

"Well we couldn't both really go, so I told Saron to. She works so hard John it will do her good."

Donna pulled John a pint.

"Do want a few sandwiches and pork pie, John? We had a pool tournament earlier and they left quite a bit of food."

"That's good of you Donna. I haven't eaten, it's been a mare of a day, only just finished work."

"Let me get you a plate and you can tell me all about it."

Donna returned with a large plate of sausage rolls, a selection of sandwiches, a pork pie and she had put a packet of crisps on the plate with some coleslaw."

"What do I owe you?"

"Nothing John, it would have been thrown away so get it down you."

John explained what had happened at work with Dirk and then today's events. He knew Donna was the sole of discretion so could speak freely to her.

It was almost 12.30am now so John thanked Donna for the food and the caring ear.

"Do you want me to tell Saron you have been in?"

"No leave it Donna, thanks again," and John left.

THE CURE

CHAPTER SEVEN

The following morning he took a call from Sergeant Beeney to tell him Andrew Gilbon had been arrested at Derby University where he worked. He had been living in the boiler house.

"Great Sergeant, I am on my way to question him."

Gammon called DCI Dirk. He didn't want to because Dirk might think he was gloating. True to form Dirk said he had concerns there was more than one killer, but he didn't share it because of morale at the station. He said he would let the powers that be know, and would be back after the weekend. That's any glory and promotion gone Gammon thought. He knew only one person was having the glory for his and Yap's efforts.

He arrived at Bixton and Beeney
had put Gilbon in interview room
one with Di Milton and DS Magic.

"Thanks, Sergeant."

Gammon dropped his laptop in his
office and went directly to interview
Gilbon whose solicitor had arrived.

Gammon entered the room. Gilbon
was unshaven and had dark Latin
type features. His solicitor was
Arthur Archer of Archer and
Kingman solicitors of Winksworth, a
noted solicitor. Gammon was quite
surprised as they tried to defend him
thirty years before in the cult bleach
case. Magic set the tape going with
the usually spiel.

"Mr Gilbon, are you aware of the
seriousness of this case?"

"No comment."

"You had administered bleach to
Jane Sharpe. Why did you do that
Mr Gilbon?"

THE CURE

"No comment."

"Ok, if we are going to play some silly game, I will set down the facts and they you may wish to change your non-cooperative stance, Mr Gilbon."

"Yesterday myself and DS Yap called to see you. We were told by the victim you were administering bleach by mouth is that correct?"

"No comment."

"She also said you kidnapped her from a bus stop."

"No comment."

At this point Arthur Archer stated that Miss Sharpe had previously beaten her client. She was clearly an aggressive assailant, so how could Mr Gilbon force Miss Sharpe to do anything he wanted?"

"Good point Mr Archer, but I am pretty sure if I put chloroform over

your airways you would not struggle
Mr Archer."

"I would recommend we take a
five minute break while you speak
with your client and let's start
moving forward."

Gammon, Magic and DI Milton
left the room and grabbed a coffee.
They waited while they drank the
coffee and then returned to the room.
DS Magic started the tape again.

"Ok Mr Gilbon, hopefully your
solicitor made you see sense. Did
you kill Jessie Toppin by
administering bleach to her?"

"No comment."

Gammon could feel the anger
inside. He hated suspects that just
played the system.

"Maga Wuxi also died when
bleach was administered to her, and
your DNA was found on her
handbag."

THE CURE

Archer butted in again.

"My client has already explained how that happened."

"Did you kill her, Mr Gilbon?"

"No comment."

"Helen Firm was also found with bleach in her body which caused her death. Did you kill her, Mr Gilbon?" Gilbon stuck with his negative approach.

"No comment."

"Now what about Mandy Bellows? Again administered bleach killed her. Were you the person that administered the bleach, Mr Gilbon?"

"No comment."

"Ok Mr Gilbon, I have heard enough, I am charging you. You do not have to say anything but …" and John carried on with the standard wording.

"The charges are as follows; kidnapping of Jane Sharpe, the charge includes holding Miss Sharpe against her will, aggravated assault, administering a known substance that could harm or kill her."

Suddenly it was like Gammon had hit a raw nerve.

"What do you know, Gammon? You know nothing of the benefits of sodium hypochlorite."

"Got you sunshine," Gammon said.

"Take him to the holding cell please, DI Milton. Oh, and get a DNA sample with John Walvin ASAP."

Gammon felt vindicated. He knew he was right, and if he could prove this idiot had a hand in all the murders he thought.

THE CURE

Gammon went to his office and wrote on his pad 'Mark Block son of David Sowers'.

He decided to go back and see Block. He drove back to Micklock Moor and Poppy Mill, home of Mark Block. Gammon arrived, and he could hear some banging in the garage, so he lifted the metal door up. To Gammon's surprise Block was welding. The welding was for a metal mask which looked grotesque. Block was shocked to see Gammon in front of him looking at the medieval mask that Block was constructing.

"Mr Block, can we have a word?"

"Yes, please follow me," Block lead Gammon into a massive kitchen with a big island in the middle. This thing must have cost a fortune Gammon thought.

Block made two coffees; one for
him and one for Gammon.

"How can I help you, Mr
Gammon?"

"Well, first of all thank you for
taking the time to come to the station
for the DNA swab. I have the results.
Would you like to know them?"

"No, I don't think so Mr
Gammon."

Gammon found the evasiveness a
little uncomfortable. What is this guy
hiding? Block seemed quite
unnerved with Gammon.

"Mr Block, I think you should
know the results of the DNA test."

Gammon felt once he told him
what the result had shown, Gammon
could then gauge the reaction.

"Ok, but I know I won't like it."

"Why not, Mr Block?"

"I was adopted at the age of three
months. I never knew my parents,

THE CURE

that is until I was ten years old. I was playing in the loft and I found some adoption papers, and they were for me. They said my mother was somebody called Margaret Summers, and my father was unknown. I never asked my adoptive parents about what I had seen. They were lovely people, and even at the age of ten, I knew telling them I knew I was adopted would have really hurt then. Many years later, I was about seventeen, we did a class on infamous people who lived or had lived in the Peak District. I really enjoyed it until my maternal mother's name came up."

"I didn't say anything to anyone, but I looked deep into the case and I saw a picture of a man with his arm round Margaret Summers. It was the cult leader, I can't remember his name, but from that day I decided to become a doctor. I do believe my mum thought she was helping mankind."

"Well let me tell you your worst fears have come to life. You are the son of David Sowers, the cult leader that poisoned your mother, and three other people."

Block crumpled in his armchair and began to weep.

"Why would my father do that to my mother, Mr Gammon?"

"I'm afraid your mum was brainwashed. Sowers was an evil egotistical man, Mr Block."

Gammon knew this poor man had nothing to do with the murders. He was a good man as everybody said, and he now had to live with his biological father being a killer."

"Mr Gammon, I am really sorry," he said wiping his eyes.

"I will be late for work."

THE CURE

"Are you going to be ok?"

"Yes, I think so. I guess deep down I always knew, but always made myself believe that it wasn't the case."

Gammon left Poppy Mill thinking how wrong he had been about Mark Block. He started his car up and left Poppy Mill. It was almost 5.00pm and was hardly worth going back to the station.

He rang DCI Dirk just to keep him in the loop. There was a lot background noise which sounded like motor bikes revving up.

"Oh, hi John, everything ok? I am just at a superbike track in Croydon with Sir Michael Brint and his son, so is it important?"

"No Sir, just keeping you up to speed on events. Give me a call tomorrow if you free."

"Ok DI Gammon," and the phone
went dead.

Bloody hell Gammon thought, any
wonder this guy gets on, he takes the
credit and rubs noses with the
hierarchy.

John decided to pick up a Chinese
on the way home and go straight
back to the cottage. He felt bad
because it was Anouska's last night.
He texted her to wish her good luck,
and to get in touch about the DNA
and what financial arrangements she
wanted putting in place once the
baby was born.

John microwaved his Chinese and
poured a large Jameson's and he sat
by the log burner. He finished his
food and promptly fell asleep,
waking up at 2.30am feeling cold.
He quickly dived into bed.

THE CURE

The following morning, feeling refreshed Gammon set off for work. He checked his phone he had a message from Anouska. It just said 'thanks'. He was almost at work when two ambulances with blue lights flashing passed him. Blimey they are in a rush he thought. Five minutes later John pulled into the car park and the two ambulances were there. Two paramedics were coming down the steps with a person in a zipped up body bag. Gammon dashed into the station. DI Smarty was standing talking to Sergeant Beeney.

"John, have you got a minute."

Smarty pulled Gammon to one side.

"Bad news mate. Gilbon has committed suicide."

"What? Are you serious? How?"

"I'm afraid Sergeant Beeney gave him a metal knife and fork. He punctured his carotid artery in his neck, first with the knife, then he opened it up with the fork. He knew what he was doing John."

"Dave, why the hell did Beeney give him metal? He knows the rules, only plastic knives and forks."

"I know John, but they brought the food to the front desk. Sergeant Beeney was on the phone and he didn't notice they hadn't brought cutlery. He couldn't leave the desk, so he gave him his own."

"Don't be too hard on him, John. It was a mistake. Gilbon would have done it at some point anyway, they always do."

"This won't be down to me Dave. They will be crawling all over this station, this is pure negligence."

THE CURE

Gammon took Beeney into a side room.

"Sergeant Beeney, you are to leave your post and not return until summoned. I am afraid this is gross misconduct is out of my hands. I need you to leave the station. You are not to have contact with any colleagues from this station. You will be summoned back here when a full a thorough investigation has been carried out."

Beeney was white and shaking.

"I'm so sorry Sir. I have let everyone down. I just didn't think."

"Please leave the building, Sergeant."

Gammon knew he could not get into a conversation with Beeney on what had happened.

Beeney left with his head down. Gammon called DI Smarty into the room.

"Who found him, Dave?"

"I did. I don't know why, but I thought I would check on him. There was blood everywhere. I rushed to get the keys from Beeney and told him to get an ambulance quickly. By the time I got to him he had left this world, his body drained of blood. The paramedics came but they knew, and put him in a body bag, and zipped him up, John."

"This will create a bloody massive shit storm Dave, and on my bloody watch as well. The media boys will love this. Ok Dave ask DS Yap to step in until this is sorted. Please mate, don't touch the cell. I best inform internal affairs."

Gammon was in two minds to ring DCI Dirk, but he had said he would call him, so he just called internal affairs.

THE CURE

"Good morning, can you put me through to internal affairs please?"

There was a second or two delay and a voice answered.

"DI Rod Allen, what's the problem?"

"Oh, good morning. This DI John Gammon at Bixton Police station Derbyshire. We have had a serious incident at the station this morning, a holding prisoner has committed suicide."

"Ok DI Gammon, we will be over with a team. Did this happen in his cell?"

"Yes, it did."

"Ok, the station is in lock down now, nobody in or out, and most definitely nobody is allowed near the scene of the suicide. Do I make myself clear?"

"Crystal, Sir."

"We will be about two hours. We are based in Hull," and the phone went dead.

Gammon followed the instructions. Luckily most of the staff were already in the building so it was just a matter of containment. Gammon could not believe his bad luck. He decided to fill his time in by nipping to see Wally to see if Gilbon's DNA had thrown anything unusual up.

"Morning John, bad news out there, mate."

"What the hell happened?"

"Long story, but Andrew Gilbon committed suicide in the holding cell. Sergeant Beeney gave him his meal and he used his steel cutlery to kill himself."

"Wow, so now we are on lockdown until when?"

THE CURE

"It will be at least four hours mate. Internal affairs won't be here for two hours, then there will be some investigating before they let us get back to something like normal."

"Anyway Wally, what about Gilbon's DNA?"

"Certainly interesting, John. Andrew Gilbon changed his name from Black to Gilbon eighteen months ago. He was the son of Donald Black, one of Sowers cult followers killed by bleach. Well that's what it seems."

"Wow, this is getting deep Wally."

"I have more for you. At the house we found letters from Walt Bellow, formerly a Bixton police officer, to Louise Black begging her not to tell anyone about what he had done. One letter says he was sorry he abused his position. He said the night he knew Donald Black was at a cult meeting he had arrested Louise Black for soliciting in a red-light area. Instead of taking her to the station he raped her then said if she ever breathed a word he would let it be known she was on the game."

"Louise took this to her grave we believe, and she didn't want her son who was born out of this devilish act to ever know his father was Walt Bellows. My guess is that killing Mandy Bellows was some kind of revenge, and maybe the bleach thing found in her was to blame it on a perceived serial killer."

"Anything else Wally?"

"Yes, we found a bank statement showing monthly monies put into her account from a William J Bellows."

"Great job again mate, plenty to go on here. Have you done with the letters?"

"All yours, John."

THE CURE

"Thanks mate, best see if the Happy Squad have arrived."

Gammon left Wally and headed to the front desk.

A tall man was standing at the front desk speaking with DS Yap.

"Sir, this is DI Rod Allen and DI Jenny Crenlin from Internal Affairs. There are also five of their officers at the holding cell."

"Ok thank you, DS Yap."

Gammon put his hand out to shake DI Allen's hand, but it wasn't reciprocated.

"DI Gammon, are you the officer in charge when the incident happened?"

"Currently DCI Dirk is in London on police business, so I generally take care of things this end."

"Ok DI Gammon, have we got a side room we can speak please?"

Gammon took them into interview room one. Rod Allen had the look of an angry man and Jenny Crenlin was a small dumpy woman in a business suit that was clearly a tight fit. She had red hair and a face that looked like she was chewing a wasp.

"DI Gammon, we need to run through some questions with you. Were you the arresting officer?"

"Yes."

"When you arrested and subsequently interviewed and then later charged Andrew Gilbon, was he showing signs of stress? Was he erratic during the interview?"

"None, I certainly didn't see any sign that you are describing. Through the interview he kept calm stating no comment to all my questions until I charged him. One of the charges was for administering sodium hypochlorite to the victim.

THE CURE

At this point he did get aggressive telling me I knew nothing of the benefits of sodium hypochlorite."

"DI Crenlin looked sternly at Gammon over her butterfly shaped red glasses.

"What happened next, DI Gammon?"

"He was taken to the holding cell."

"When did he take his own life?"

"I'm not sure of the time but they usually serve breakfast about 7.45am to the holding cells."

"Who found the man?"

"DI Dave Smarty, he had just gone to check on him."

"What did he use to cut his neck artery?"

"A knife and a fork."

"What, a plastic knife and fork?"

John knew his next answer would throw poor Sergeant Beeney under the bus.

"No, a metal knife and fork to eat his breakfast with."

"What sort of station are you running here Gammon? Do you not know the rules about anything that a prisoner can harm himself with, but you allow metal implements into a cell?"

"We always use plastic, but from what Sergeant Beeney said the kitchen staff forgot to bring the prisoner his cutlery. Sergeant Beeney was really busy so he gave him a metal set that was at the front desk. It wasn't intentional it was a genuine mistake."

"We will be the judge of that Gammon. It was certainly stupid on Sergeant Beeney's behalf. Where is Beeney now?"

"I sent him home and told him we would call him in, but in between time he wasn't to have contact with any of his colleagues at Bixton station."

"Ok Gammon, we have done with you for now. Get DI Smarty to come in here."

Ignorant git John thought.

"Before I go, how long will the station be on lock-down?"

"Until I tell you otherwise, DI Gammon."

Gammon got DI Smarty.

"Just be careful Dave, it isn't looking good for young Beeney."

"Ok John."

Gammon went to his office and sat doing some reports. Eventually Jenny Crenlin came to his office.

"Ok DI Gammon, you can re-open the station, but arrange for Sergeant Beeney to attend a meeting with myself and DI Allen at 9.00am. Gammon felt like pushing her down the stairs, arrogant cow he thought.

He called Beeney and he sounded very nervous.

"Will they throw me off the force, Sir?"

"I can't discuss anything with you Warren, I'm sorry. Just make sure you are here for 9.00am please."

Gammon ended the call and decided he best let DCI Dirk know what happened. After three attempts he finally got through. Gammon filled DCI Dirk in. To say he was miffed was an understatement. This would not look good on his CV Gammon thought. Dirk clearly hadn't got an ounce of compassion for poor Beeney. He was more concerned about his own neck.

Dirk told Gammon he would be back in the morning. Gammon let DS Yap know the station was open for business, so he could tell everyone.

THE CURE

"They all just left, Sir."

"Have you had to book some accommodation for them?"

"Yes, Allen and Crenlin are at the Spinning Jenny and the other five are staying at the Wobbly Man in Toad Holes."

Great John thought. Now he thought he would avoid the Spinning Jenny if that pair were going to be staying there.

He stood looking at Losehill unsure of anything anymore. He was to be a dad but only in the financial sense. Saron blew hot and cold

And if she found out about the baby that was possibly conceived the night before their wedding, then hell would freeze over before she would talk to him again. He had Steve to support, although he didn't seem too bad. What a mess he thought now this.

Gammon sat down and scribbled on his pad. Gilbon possibly killed Mandy Bellows because of her father Walt, so he had to get him in for questioning. Mark Block, he was happy to cross off his list. The problem was something was niggling him about the whole case. Jessie Toppin had been murdered by Sowers, and there was no doubt about that.

Helen Firm, had he been a bit too quick to dismiss Andrew Firm as a suspect? He was quite sure that Gilbon murdered Mandy Bellows and also Maga Wuxi. The other one he wasn't sure about, Helen Firm, was found with extensive punctures in her arm so the bleach had been injected but why? Was the killer a doctor perhaps?

John wrote on his pad 'Cult'? Then he sat thinking Block's father was Sowers. Gilbon's mother was Louise Black, but his real father was Walt Bellows hence the murder of Mandy Bellows. They were all intertwined. Was there a cult carrying on the work of Sowers and Jackie Bush through various kids? If so, where did Helen Firm fit in. Gammon decided he would see if Yvette Wyn or Ivan Wilson had any connection to Helen Firm. He called down to Wally to see if Wyn or Wilson had any DNA on record, and if Helen Firm's DNA matched.

"It won't be tonight mate."

"No, that's ok. Have a look for me tomorrow please."

"Will do, John."

Gammon knew this was a long shot, but he had nothing else. He rang Walt Bellows to come to the station to be interviewed in the morning. Walt asked Gammon what was it about?

"I will see you tomorrow. I suggest you bring a solicitor. If you could be here for 9.00am please."

Walt Bellows agreed but seemed a bit confused with the request.

It was 6.40pm so John shut down his laptop and headed out.

John arrived for a quick pint at the Spinning Jenny, but as soon as he walked in he remembered DI Allen and DI Crenlin were staying there. He quickly scanned the bar area but could only see Kev, so he took a chance and carried onto the bar.

"Evening Kev, how are you mate?"

"Not good John. I just find a new bar maid and flippin Anouska has left to go home. I can't weigh it up. I thought she liked it here, and she certainly liked you."

THE CURE

Doreen heard the conversation as she came down the corridor.

"I want a word with you young John," and she hauled him over to the window seat.

"What's up Doreen, this looks serious."

"You have heard Anouska has gone home."

"Yeah Kev just said."

"Any idea why?"

"No, why would I?"

Doreen pulled out a used pregnancy kit from her pocket.

"I found this in her draw in her bedroom. Now counting back you don't have to be a mathematician to work this out John, do you?"

John could feel is face going scarlet.

"It's yours, isn't it? You can't lie to me John. I have known you too long."

"Ok Doreen, she is going to have a DNA test, but yes pretty sure it's mine."

"You bloody fool. I told you she was trouble but you, and that dickie bowed lump I call my husband, ignored me.

"What are you going to do if people work this out. They will know, and Saron will certainly know that this was probably on the eve of your wedding."

"Anouska has told me she isn't coming back. If the DNA results she sends me are correct, then I will support my child."

"Well good luck with that one, she will want more. More won't be enough, and I will be proved right again. Your secret is safe with me John. I just wish Kev hadn't employed her."

THE CURE

With that Doreen went back to the kitchen and John went back to the bar.

"What did my good lady want you for, all secretive like?"

"Sure she will tell you if you ask Kev."

"Don't look so down."

John never talked about work, but he told Kev what had happened.

"Doesn't sound too good for your Sergeant."

"I think the Internal Affairs officers are staying here, Kev."

"Oh, a tall guy with a really aggressive look and a small dumpy woman with ginger hair."

"That's them."

"I think they are booked in the restaurant for a meal at 8.00pm."

Kev had no sooner got the words out of his mouth when Jenny Crenlin came into the bar area. She had

changed into a black suit with
trousers, and now she had a pair of
butterfly shaped glasses, but this
time they were purple.

"DI Gammon, have you not seen
enough of myself and DI Allen
today?"

John bit his tongue and just
smiled. Through gritted teeth he
asked Crenlin if she would like a
drink.

"A large gin and tonic, ice but no
slice, and I will pay for my own
drink, DI Gammon. It's against the
rules," and she glared at John.

"Landlord, give me a pint of that
beer there."

"Pedigree?"

"Yes, whatever it is. My colleague
will be down in a minute. Could you
take them to my table in your
restaurant?"

THE CURE

"Goodnight, DI Gammon," and she waltzed of with her nose in the air. Kev looked at John.

"Pity poor Beeney, John. She is after blood mate."

"Tell me about it."

John had one more pint then left for the night. The nights were starting to get lighter, so he took a different route down through Lingcliffe into Pritwich with its quaint church and duck pond. Then he climbed out through Hittington then Hitting on the Dale and arriving home at 9.22pm.

It was so peaceful down at the farm cottages. He poured a Jameson's and sat in the garden watching two squirrels playing. There was a good selection of birds singing and the garden felt idyllic. He sat pondering. He knew deep down that Sergeant Beeney would either be demoted to the beat, or in the worst case be thrown off the force. In John eyes this was a waste, just for a stupid mistake. Gilbon would have found an opportunity just like Sowers did.

Finally it started to turn quite cool, so John headed for bed. He was reading a book called 'I am Fawn Jones' from an author called Colin J Galtrey. It was a bit detective and a bit about people on the other side that had died. They were trying to get through to their parents to tell them who the killer was. John read fifty pages, and as much as he wanted to carry on as it was getting intriguing, he could not keep his eyes open.

The following morning he showered and set off for work. DCI Dirk was back so he wanted to remind him he would be away the week after next for his holiday with Steve.

Gammon arrived at the station.

"Morning Sir."

"Be glad when this is all over, so I can carry on in my detective job."

"Understand Ian, let's hope they are lenient with Sergeant Beeney."

DCI Dirk was in his office. Gammon expected him to quite irate, but he was remarkably calm. Take a seat John. He was just about to start when his desk phone rang.

"Good morning, Commissioner."

"Yes, back to steady the ship. The cutlery thing? Yes Sir, it's another one that needs my attention, but we are making improvements all round. I'm afraid it is looking like the Sergeant involved will be dismissed. I'm sure we can find another desk Sergeant the good name of the station must prevail. I will Sir and thank you for calling. Oh, before you go Sir, are you attending the October ball at the Grosvenor, and the shoot at Lord Digglebury's estate the next day. Yes, it is a long way in front Sir, but that's me. Dot every I and cross every T Sir. Lovely to talk to you, Commissioner. Have a splendid day."

John realised that Dirk was very well connected and that a deal had been done with Internal Affairs to ensure that Beeney was the scapegoat. Nothing was sticking to him and secondly to Bixton police station.

"Did you want something, DI Gammon?"

John smiled and said no and left. In all the years he had been in the force he actually felt ashamed to be a policeman. There was absolutely no thought to a genuine mistake that Beeney made with a scumbag that had possibly murdered two women then committed suicide. What was policing coming to he thought, as he made his way to his office leaving Dirk to sit in with Internal affairs and dismiss Beeney.

Gammon was expecting Anouska to come back with the pre-natal paternity test results. She had asked him to send his DNA which he had done with a mouth swab. A bit of him was excited, but she had the bigger job with wanting to know before the baby was born.

DI Milton called to give John the bad news about poor Beeney.

"Hey John."

"Why, is it done?"

"Yeah, they have finished him on gross misconduct. The union rep said he had no chance of winning if he takes it further. He left here in a real state mate. I thought about going to see him but don't want to get tarred with the same brush."

"Best leave it Carl, there is nothing we can do."

DI Scooper said DCI Dirk was laughing and shaking hands with the two Internal Affairs as they left.

"The decision wasn't ours Carl. We just have to get on. How are you?"

"If you mean because of Beth, then I am ok John. I have to forget her and move on. I was hoping to take Anouska out, but I saw Kev at the paper shop and he said she had gone home and wasn't coming back."

Gammon quickly changed the subject and told Carl he had to crack on as Walt Bellows had arrived. John took DI Scooper to work the tape machine and DI Smarty to the interview. Yap had them put in interview room two.

Scooper set the tape going and Gammon introduced everyone in the room. Bellows said Michael Foss was his solicitor representing him.

"What is this about, DI Gammon?"

"Well we apprehended a man yesterday that we believe murdered your daughter, Mr Bellows. During our investigations and a subsequent search of his house we believe you may be the father of the man."

"Don't be stupid Mr Gammon. I had a daughter, that was my only child."

"So you won't mind doing a DNA test, so we can disprove the letter we found at this man's house."

Bellows wasn't stupid, but he agreed reluctantly.

Gammon sent DI Smarty to get somebody to do a DNA test on Bellows.

"We believe that Andrew Gilbon was your love child with Louise Black."

"You needn't bother to do the DNA test. Andrew Gilbon as you call him was my son."

"Are the letters correct, that you raped Louise Black?"

"Louise was on the game. Her husband Donald Black was a member of Sowers cult."

Walt Bellows put his head in his hands, shaking his head and weeping. Gammon offered him a glass of water.

"I am so ashamed. Thirty odd years ago coppers often went with the prostitutes, I was no different. I didn't rape her. It was like an unwritten law, but because she hadn't been on the game longer, she said I had forced myself on her. I got annoyed. I couldn't have her telling anyone or I would lose my job. A few months went by and I decided to go down to where I had met her. A working girl said she had got herself pregnant. I only saw her one more time, but I did send those letters. To this day I feel dreadful about what I did. Now you tell me that mistake thirty odd years ago meant my beautiful daughter was murdered by my illegitimate son because of those bloody letters."

"What now Mr Gammon?"

"I think you have paid the price for your indiscretions and I doubt the CPS would allow what you did go to trial. You having to live with it, this is justice enough Mr Bellows. You are free to go."

Bellows hung his head in shame as he left the station.

So, with Andrew Gilbon having murdered Mega Wuxi and Mandy Bellows, and attempted the same with Jane David Sowers take the blame for Sharpe who luckily survived. It was Gammon's guess that he used the bleach in some kind of experiment and Sowers was probably his mentor having shown him with the death of Jessie Toppin. That still left Helen Firm.

Gammon went to see Wally to check if any DNA was found that might incriminate Andrew Gilbon. His thought was Gilbon killed Mandy Bellows in spite towards his real father Walt Bellows. He killed Magi Wuxi, and Jessie Toppin as part of some bizarre experiment. Although it was hard to prove, but after an altercation with Helen Firm, he used her on the experiment with the bleach.

A couple of hours passed and Wally rang.

"Sorry mate, nothing on the DNA. I had checked before but always worth checking again."

"No problem mate."

Gammon informed DCI Dirk of his findings and he couldn't wait to let the hierarchy know. Of course for the glory that came with it.

A week passed and it was Sunday night. John had a small case packed. Steve said he would pick him up at 4.00am and he wanted to drive up to Scotland. The plan was to have an over-night stay in Edinburgh.

John set his alarm for 3.00am and now that the cases seemed closed he slept a bit better. Although he knew that next week Anouska would probably be in touch about the DNA result.

Steve arrived in his Porsche Cayan, all shiny, he seemed very pleased with it. They chatted all the way to Edinburgh and they had booked into a Holiday Inn. Once they had checked in and dropped their things in the rooms they decided to go and have a breakfast.

"I am starving John, don't know about you?"

"Could eat a horse then go back for the jockey mate."

They walked for about a quarter of a mile and found The Bacon Butty, a small deli type café.

"Come on mate this will do."

They both ordered a big breakfast. John had just taken a mouthful of sausage and his phone rang.

"That can wait, Steve."

THE CURE

It constantly kept ringing through breakfast.

"Bloody hell."

John answered the mobile. It was DCI Dirk.

"Where are you, Gammon?"

"I'm in Edinburgh, Sir."

"Get your arse back here. We have had a dual murder sometime last night, and it looks like your bleach killer is still at large."

John decided to stand his ground on this.

"I am on holiday, Sir."

"If you don't get back here now you will be on permanent holiday. This is embarrassing for the station and myself," and the phone went dead.

"I don't believe this guy."

John told Steve what he had said.

"Well actually mate, this might be a good opportunity. You know I want to build the house back up in memory of Jo and Leah. Well why don't you jack all that crap in? Come in with me. We build it and have it as a luxury spar and hotel and run it together."

"Mate, I love my job, even working with arse-holes like him."

"All I am saying mate, is think about it."

"Let's get back I suppose. Sorry for ruining your break. I can go back on the train mate."

"No, it won't be the same. I'll take you back. But think about what I have said. I have all the plans. We can sit and look at them one night."

"Ok mate"

They arrived back at Bixton and Steve dropped John off. It was almost 2.00pm. He was feeling really aggrieved so went straight to DCI Dirk's office to have it out with him.

THE CURE

There was nobody in the office, so he went back down to ask Sergeant Yap.

"He's gone home poorly, Sir. He didn't think he would be back all week. He was going to bed he said."

Bloody moron John thought. That's why he wanted me back.

"DS Yap, can you get Scooper, Smarty, Lee, Milton and DS Magic in the incident room right away please?"

"Will do, Sir."

Gammon was feeling so annoyed, but it wasn't Yap's fault so as he left he apologised for his manner.

The team were assembled.

"Thought you were away for the week, Sir?"

"I was Magic, but that's another story. Can you get me up to speed on the latest two victims?"

DI Smarty stood.

"At around midnight on Sunday the station took a call from a male. He said he will never be defeated. One day sodium hypochlorite will be proven to cure many ills that the fat cat pharmaceutical companies have conned you all for many years. Our work carries on. Like all things you have to crack an egg to make an omelette, and the victims willingly took part. Sadly, Simone Corrigan and Hatty Corrigan will one day be called martyrs. You will find their bodies at the back of the Sycamore in Pritwich, behind the clothing collection point in the car-park. The man then hung up. Trimble called me, and I got DI Lee, and we went and found the bodies. Wally's team were called in. He confirmed at lunch they died from sodium hypochlorite. He has found no DNA other than their own. He did comment that they he thought they were twins."

"Ok, has anybody been to see their parents?"

"I was going now that Wally confirmed."

"Ok Dave, I'll come with you."

Smarty and Gammon left the meeting and headed to Pritwich. They followed the hill down past DI Scooper's cottage and the magnificent hall her mother still lived at, the duck pond, the pub and the shop. They followed the lane at the side of the beautiful village church, finally arriving at Crook Stile cottage. An elderly couple were tending their garden. They both looked that they must have been retired.

"Good afternoon, Mr and Mrs Corrigan?"

"Yes, how can we help you?"

"Could we have a word please?" Gammon and Smarty showed their warrant cards.

"Please do come in," said the sprightly older lady.

"Would you like a cup of tea and a piece of my fruit loaf perhaps?"

"We'll take the tea, but no fruit loaf for us thank you, Mrs Corrigan."

"Oh, I'm not Mrs Corrigan. She died just after the twins were born. Cancer sadly, wasn't it, Sydney?

"Yes, the doctors tried everything."

"Oh, I'm Yvette Wyn."

Gammon took a deep breath. He knew the name, but he hadn't come to question Yvette Wyn. He had come with the grave news about Mr Corrigan's twins.

She brought the tea through and they sat in the living room.

"How can we help you?"

THE CURE

"I said to Yvette around midnight last night that something had gone on at the Sycamore. There were blue flashing lights. I had just taken the dog out. She is getting old now like us and can't hold herself. She has to go every six or so hours Mr Gammon."

Gammon knew this was going to be difficult but there was no easy way.

"You have two daughters, Mr Corrigan?"

"Please call me Stan."

"Ok Stan. Your daughters."

"Yes, Simone and Hatty, they are studying at Derby University. They both want to be chemists."

"Mr Corrigan, I am sorry to tell you both girls were found dead this morning in the Sycamore car park."

Stan Corrigan just looked aghast at Gammon. Yvette comforted him.

"Yvette, I have to ask this. Your name is synonymous with the cult killings thirty odd years back."

"Yes, that was my mum. My father brought me up. I was christened Julia, but everyone called me Yvette after mum because they said I looked like her."

Gammon didn't push this any further. It wasn't the time or the place, but certainly a coincidence of some magnitude.

"I am sorry to ask you this Stan, but you will need to come and identify the bodies about 11.00am tomorrow. Will you need picking up?"

"I will drive him there, Mr Gammon."

"Ok Yvette, here is my card, if you require anything call me anytime."

THE CURE

Gammon drove back to the station thinking it seemed strange that Yvette Wyn lived with the man whose twin daughters had been murdered. Her mother was part of the sect thirty years previous that appeared to be reinventing itself through children of the sect. There was something in all this that would make sense eventually. Too much pointed to the bleach cure he thought.

To be continued ……

JOHN GAMMON PEAK DISTRICT DETECTIVE
Series Three Book Two

DI John Gammon series one

BOOK ONE: THINGS WILL NEVER BE THE SAME AGAIN.
BOOK TWO: SAD MAN
BOOK THREE: JOY FOLLOWS SORROW
BOOK FOUR: NEVER CRY ON A BLUEBELL
BOOK FIVE: ANNIE TANNEY

DI John Gammon series two

BOOK ONE: THE POET AND THE CALLING CARD
BOOK TWO: WHY
BOOK THREE: YOUR PAST IS YOUR FUTURE
BOOK FOUR: INTRAVENOUS
BOOK FIVE: THE SORROW FOLLOWS

DI John Gammon series three

BOOK ONE: THE MAGPIE
BOOK TWO: THE CURE

THE CURE

Other genres

A trilogy of love stories/time travel and dreams

BOOK ONE: LOOKING FOR SHONA
BOOK TWO: THE HURT OF YOCHANA
BOOK THREE: GROVE

A thriller

BOOK ONE: GOT TO KEEP RUNNING

A thriller involving the after life

BOOK ONE: I AM FAWN JONES